# The Death Club

or

## The Case of the Ebony Skulls

## by G. H. Teed

Illustrated by Val Reading
and Francis H. Warren

First published in The Union Jack Library,
Special Double Summer Number,
Series 2, No. 558, 20 June 1914.

Stillwoods Edition

*Stillwoods.Blogspot.Ca*

**Catalogue Information:**
Title: The Death Club
Subtitle: The Case of the Ebony Skulls.
Author: G. H. Teed (1881-1938)
Illustrated by: Val Reading and Francis H. Warren.
First published anonymously in The Union Jack Library, Special Double Summer Number, Series 2, No. 558, 20 June 1914.
This Edition by: Stillwoods, 2021
ISBN Canada: 978-1-989788-68-4
Blog: Stillwoods.Blogspot.Ca
Author Blog: http://ghteed.blogspot.com/
**Storefront: http://www.lulu.com/spotlight/lulubook22**

**Teed Bibliography Link:**
https://tinyurl.com/ve25d42s
The link above should go to a spreadsheet of all known Teed stories. The list is annotated with various information on the stories and my progress with recapturing the work.   /drf

The library of Teed's stories increases almost daily. Check at the storefront link above for the latest arrivals. /drf

Keywords: Sexton Blake, British fictional detective, Tinker, Yvonne Cartier, Uncle Graves, Mr. Hammerton Palmer.

**Cautionary Note:** This series of books by Stillwoods are intended to make the stories of G. H. Teed, born in New Brunswick, Canada, available to collectors and researchers. The editor, or rather digitizer has not intentionally altered the original publication.

This story may contain language and racial terms that are not appropriate to today. I apologize for them; I know that the author was using his voice to excite and entertain an adventurous English audience. These works were published from 82 to 110 years ago. Most every work has characters of redeeming ethnicity within.

I hope you enjoy and share these stories; I have.

Doug Frizzle

THE UNION JACK LIBRARY
Special Summer Number.

# THE DEATH CLUB.

A Detective Romance Specially
Written to Appeal to All Tastes,
All Ages—Either Sex.

### CAST.

Mdlle. YVONNE - The Charming Adventuress.
GRAVES - - - - - Her Uncle.
Mr. HAMMERTON PALMER - Financier.
Mr. GILBERT JEFFERSON - Silk Merchant.
ALICE JEFFERSON - - Jefferson's Niece.
FORMBY MOTT - - - - Lawyer.
HERBERT CHANNING - Yvonne's Agent.
Inspector THOMAS - - of Scotland Yard.
TINKER - - - - Boy Detective.

... AND ...

## SEXTON BLAKE—Detective.

FRANCIS H. WARREN.

Illustrations
by
"VAL,"
and
FRANCIS
H.
WARREN.

No. 558.          June 20th, 1914.          EVERY THURSDAY.

A Detective Romance Specially Written to Appeal to All Tastes, All Ages —Either Sex.

CAST.

Mdlle. YVONNE - The Channing Adventuress.

GRAVES - Her Uncle.

Mr. HAMMERTON PALMER - Financier.

Mr. GILBERT JEFFERSON - Silk Merchant.

ALICE JEFFERSON - Jefferson's Niece.

FORMBY MOTT - Lawyer.

HERBERT CHANNING - Yvonne's Agent.

Inspector THOMAS - of Scotland Yard.

TINKER - Boy Detective.

AND ...

SEXTON BLAKE - Detective.

This special summer issue features an extra long story and profusely illustrated.

# THE DEATH CLUB

## Or, THE CASE OF THE EBONY SKULLS.

MADEMOISELLE YVONNE lighted a tiny cigarette and leaned back in a negligent attitude, the while she calmly studied the features of the young man who sat in the chair facing her. Outside, the belated spring was drenching London with an ardent downpour, as though still to keep fresh in the minds of the inhabitants the memory of the dismal winter.

Yvonne and her guest were sitting before a cheerful fire in the study in Yvonne's apartment at Queen Anne's Gate, and on such a night it seemed a particularly cosy retreat.

The young man was neither prepossessing nor insignificant in appearance. Rather was he the thin, pale, slightly stooped bespectacled type which spoke of long hours spent in bending over a desk. And in this case appearances were not deceptive.

He had, in truth, spent a good part of his still young life in that occupation. Starting as a bookkeeper, Herbert Channing had toiled incessantly until he had become worthy of far better things than a clerkship and two pounds a week.

It was then that the investigation of the affairs of a certain City firm, which was in the market for more capital, had brought Channing to Yvonne's notice. She had taken note of the exceptional neatness and elaborate detail of his work, and when the extension of her interests demanded that she should have a trustworthy and competent auditor, she had sent for Channing.

Nor had she been disappointed in her judgment of his ability. Under her he had developed to a marked degree that inherent capacity which in his other sphere had been cramped and stifled. Left to himself and his own initiative, he had put into practice the ideas which had rested dormant in his mind, until, to-day he was one of the shrewdest and most competent auditors in the City.

From his former two pounds a week he had jumped to twenty, and as his material fortunes had advanced, so had his loyalty and devotion increased for the one who had given him his chance.

The work he did for Yvonne was varied in the extreme. To-day he might be posing as a clerk at thirty shillings a week in some mercantile house which was seeking capital. To-morrow he might be acting as paymaster in some gold or copper mine in Nevada or Australia. But wherever he was or whatever he was doing, he was acting for Yvonne, and on his report did she invariably act.

Evidently his call on her this stormy April night was to present to her the results of some investigation on her behalf, for on his knee lay a very thick blue envelope. And a moment later Yvonne's words proved this to be so.

"I hardly expected you to finish before the end of the month, Mr. Channing," she said, as she puffed lazily at her cigarette.

"To tell you the truth, I thought it would take that long, too, Mademoiselle Yvonne," replied Channing. "I was able, however, to gain access to the private ledgers much sooner than I expected, and this helped a lot. I have made out a detailed report of the firm's condition. It is here in this envelope, and I think you will find it covers all the ground —at least, it deals with every phase of the firm's existence during the past two years. That was the length of time you wished covered."

Yvonne nodded.

"Yes. I had a report on it for the period of its existence preceding that. It was just two years ago that I invested in it."

"I saw the account of your investment —fifty thousand pounds."

"What is the sum and substance of what you discovered?"

"Well, in a way you were right, and, in a way, wrong in your suspicions, mademoiselle.

"To begin with, from the time of your investment the firm seems to have expanded wonderfully, proving that all it needed was additional capital. Your judgment on that point was excellent. Furthermore, when, through you, it got rid of its retail shops, and concentrated on the wholesaling of silk only, its turnover, though less in the gross, shows a far greater net profit —due, in great part, to a consequent reduction in working expenses.

"To-day, of course, the Jefferson Silk Company is the standard firm for high-grade silks. On the other hand, your suspicions that Gilbert Jefferson, the president, had been gambling heavily on the Stock Exchange were well founded. His private ledger, which I was enabled to examine, shows several large transactions with two different firms.

"These operations began shortly after your investment in the firm, and from that date on, until seven months ago, his own private account shows a constantly growing overdraft. Then all record of his stock gambling transactions stop. Moreover, his personal account begins then to show big credits.

"In fact, at the date I speak of, seven months, ago, his unsecured overdraft amounted to forty thousand pounds, and, from the condition of the other accounts, it is evident to me that he must have been discovered before long. Neither the firm nor himself could stand the strain.

"Then the very next month his account shows that eight thousand pounds was paid into it; the next, seven thousand five hundred; the next, ten thousand; the next, six thousand five hundred; the next, three thousand; the next, another three thousand; and last month, an even five thousand.

"Strangely enough, I can find absolutely no trace of any memorandum or transaction to account for his receipt of these large sums. It seems almost as though he had made several huge deals on the Stock Exchange in a desperate attempt to get square, and had succeeded.

"At the same time, that does not explain the reason his private ledger shows no record of a Stock Exchange transaction during the past seven months. But you can see that up to last month he was quite square —in fact, had a credit of three thousand pounds."

"You interest me exceedingly," remarked Yvonne, as Channing paused. "Did you find all purchase and sales records correct? Might it be possible that he has been juggling with the stocks of silk?"

"That occurred to me, and I went into the question at once. An exhaustive investigation shows that the whole business of the firm is quite regular, and in a most healthy condition."

"Peculiar," murmured Yvonne. "I knew Jefferson was gambling heavily in stocks, and suspected that the business would be the sufferer from it. Knowing how reckless he was becoming, it seems odd that he should stop so suddenly.

"Then the huge monthly receipts from that time on are most puzzling. From what you can find out, it seems that they come from a source outside the company?"

"Absolutely. I am sure, mademoiselle."

"Did you run across anything else?"

"Yes, I did, and that is what I wish to speak of now. On examining the contents of the safe, I discovered four things of interest, mademoiselle. Two of those things were insurance policies on the life of Gilbert Jefferson. They were for ten thousand pounds each. One of them was dated two years ago, and was made payable to the Jefferson Silk Company."

"I know about that. I insisted on Jefferson becoming insured for that amount when I put money in the firm. But go on."

"The other was for ten thousand pounds, too. It was made seven months ago, and was made payable—to whom do you think?"

"I can't guess."

"To Hammerton Palmer, the wealthy financier. The third I discovered in the safe was a short will dated just seven months ago. It confirmed the leaving of the policy for ten thousand to Hammerton Palmer, and, in addition to that, left him half his interest in the Jefferson Silk Company —or, roughly, shares worth easily thirty thousand pounds.

"That makes forty thousand pounds he intends leaving to Hammerton Palmer, and he specified most clearly that it is left in recognition and in payment of value received during his lifetime from Hammerton Palmer. The balance of his estate he leaves in trust for his niece.

"The fourth thing of interest which I found in the safe was a memorandum, which was dated only yesterday, and which said:

" 'Charge personal account with twenty thousand pounds. In event of my death before repayment to be repaid by life policy for ten thousand already made payable to company, and ten thousand pounds in shares to be taken from those left in my will to my niece. None of money or shares left to Hammerton Palmer to be touched.'"

"And you say that was only dated yesterday?" asked Yvonne sharply.

"Yes. It was signed and witnessed by the head clerk and one of the other clerks."

Yvonne bent forward and drew a pad towards her. Picking up a pencil she wrote busily for a few moments; then she looked up.

"This is a rough statement of what I gather from your verbal report," she said,

"Firstly, that seven months ago, Gilbert Jefferson was overdrawn on his private account with the Jefferson Silk Company, to the extent of forty thousand pounds, due to heavy gambling on the Stock Exchange. Then he apparently stops gambling, and, instead of his account showing further debits, it begins to show large monthly credits.

"At the same time, he takes out an insurance policy for ten thousand pounds. Also he makes a will. Both the policy and the will —the former entirely and the latter partially —are in favour of Hammerton Palmer, the financier. They total together forty thousand pounds, or roughly the amount he was overdrawn seven months ago.

"In addition to this, the monthly sums he has paid in during that seven months pay back this forty thousand pounds overdraft, and leave about three thousand to the good. In other words, seven months ago the company must have been on the brink of ruin, regardless of the healthy condition of its turnover. Now it is quite sound again.

"Further, his will reads that the amounts left to Hammerton Palmer are for 'value received.' That looks almost as though the forty thousand odd pounds, which he has repaid, came from Hammerton Palmer.

"Now we come to a peculiar thing. I speak of the memorandum showing that he drew twenty thousand pounds of the firm's money only yesterday. Why did he require such a large sum of money as that? For what purpose? Is it possible that, now his overdraft has been repaid, he is beginning to gamble on the Stock Exchange again? If that is so he must be stopped at once before he brings the company where he brought it before.

"Last month he was square, and had three thousand pounds to his credit. Now he is seventeen thousand pounds over-drawn again. If the insurance policy and the thirty thousand pounds in shares are to go to Hammerton Palmer, that leaves thirty thousand pounds in shares to go to his niece, for his interest in the company amounts to sixty thousand exactly.

"Supposing he should be overdrawn another forty thousand. His niece's share and the policy for ten thousand would just cover it. That would leave his niece penniless, for, naturally, the firm would demand the payment of the overdraft. In any case, it is not well, and, as I said, it must be stopped."

"You have stated the case exactly as it is, mademoiselle. I can find no record that he is possessed of any other property."

"If you will leave the report I shall not detain you any longer to-night," said Yvonne alter a short pause. "I am very pleased with your prompt completion of the investigation, Mr. Channing. It is just possible I may want you to go out on another matter in a few days; in any event, I shall let you know, and your salary continues as usual."

"Thank you, Mademoiselle Yvonne," answered Channing rising. "I hope you will have something else soon. I like to keep busy."

"All right," she smiled. "I shall remember."

A moment later he was gone, and Yvonne sat poring over the complicated report which he had brought. It was close on eleven o'clock when the door opened and Graves her uncle, entered. His damp boots showed that he had but just come in out of the rain.

Yvonne looked up with a smile.

"You are home early, uncle? Was the card-room at the club deserted this evening?"

Graves sank down before the open fire with a sigh of relief.

"Yes. It was deadly. Everybody seems to have cleared out to a better climate, though it is April. What do you say to a little jaunt ourselves?"

"I say you had better change your boots before you get cold," laughed Yvonne, "You know what a bear you are when you are not well."

"I am going in a minute. But how about a trip?"

"Impossible! I am too busy."

"What's on now, Yvonne?"

"Nothing much. Channing has been here to bring a report and I have been going through it. By the way, when you get up to change your boots, ring the garage on the 'phone, and tell Alec to bring the limousine round at once, there's a dear."

"The limousine!" ejaculated Graves. "What on earth do you want with the car at this time of night?"

"I am going out. But I won't be long."

"Where are you going? Can't you put it off until to-morrow?"

"I could, but I think it is a case where prompt action may be of value. I propose making a quiet investigation of the desk and safe, if there is one, in the house of a certain gentleman."

"You'd better go easy, Yvonne. You know the police have by no means forgotten your past exploits, and if you were caught it would be deucedly awkward."

"Oh! I can take care of myself all right. But go along now and put on a dry pair of shoes. I suppose you will wait up for me?"

Graves, who was on his way to the door, stopped.

"Of course. Where is it you are going, and how long do you expect to be gone?"

6

"I am going to pay a midnight visit to the house of Gilbert Jefferson and —why, what is the matter, uncle?"

Yvonne broke oft and started to her feet, as she saw Graves swing sharply and exhibit a suddenly ashen face.

"You—are— going—where?" he gasped, feeling mechanically for his collar as though he would loosen it.

"To the house of Gilbert Jefferson," answered Yvonne.

Graves staggered to the table and leaned heavily against it. His knuckles stood out white, and the pallor of his cheeks matched the white of his beard.

"But no —no, Yvonne," he finally jerked. "You must not go there. Not to-night. Wait until to-morrow. Not to-night —not to-night."

Yvonne stepped forward swiftly and laid a hand on his arm.

"Why, uncle?" she said looking up at him, "this is not a bit like you. Why should the mention of Gilbert Jefferson's name affect you in this way? Why should I not enter his house to-night? I did not know you had ever met him."

"Nor have I," stammered Graves.

"Then it is something else which has affected you," she cried anxiously. "Is it a sudden seizure —is it your heart? Tell me what is wrong, uncle?"

Graves licked his dry lips,

"It is nothing, Yvonne. Only don't —don't go to Gilbert Jefferson's house to-night. Wait until to-morrow."

"But uncle, he almost wrecked the Jefferson Silk Company once. I put Channing in there as a clerk in order to find out how things stood at present. Although the old condition has been restored during the past seven months, there are signs that Jefferson is tampering with the firm's resources again.

"If he has entered into any Stock Exchange deals he must have some memoranda of them. They are not in the safe at the offices of the company, therefore, I argue they must be at his house. That is what I wish to discover. You know I am perfectly capable of entering his house and getting away again without being discovered.

"But even if he should surprise me I shouldn't mind much. It would be a good opportunity to have a quiet talk with him. I am determined to stop him from gambling with the funds of the company."

"Is that what that report is about?"

"Yes."

"It won't make much difference to wait until to-morrow. It can't be is urgent as that. Wait, I beg of you, Yvonne, wait until the morning. I have a particular reason for asking."

Yvonne drew back and studied him curiously.

"I am entirely unable to understand you, uncle," she said coldly. "Why can't you be frank? You say you have a particular reason for wishing me to stay home to-night. You said nothing to that effect until I mentioned Gilbert Jefferson's name. Then you behaved in a very strange manner.

"Yet you say you never met him. Then why should you be so affected by the mention of his name? This is not like you, uncle. We have always had perfect frankness between us. Why do you conceal something now? Come!

"If you can tell me any good reason why I should not carry out my purpose to-night, then I promise you, before hearing it, that I shall remain at home and wait until to-morrow. If not, then I shall go."

"Oh, my heavens!" groaned Graves sinking into a chair. "Listen, Yvonne," he went on pleadingly. "Don't ask me to explain my reason. Believe me, my dear, I would if I could. But trust me. Don't go to Gilbert Jefferson's house to-night, I can't say more —I know a reason why you should not, but my lips are sealed."

Yvonne straightened up and took the report from the table. She was humming softly to herself, and apparently oblivious now of her uncle's presence in the room —both a sure indication that she was feeling intensely angry.

She locked the report in a drawer of the desk, then, taking the 'phone, called the garage. In a few terse words she ordered Alec the chauffeur to bring round the limousine. After that she rose and made for the door, but Graves was before her, barring her way.

"Listen, Yvonne," he said hoarsely. "I can see you are determined on going there. If you are I know it is useless to try to stop you. At least, however, let me go with you."

"I am sorry, but I must go alone," answered Yvonne briefly. "It is a thing which is safe for one to attempt but dangerous for two."

"Then —then promise me this. If you see lights in the house, or any signs of commotion about the place, don't make the attempt to-night. Will you promise that?"

"Certainly. I should not try to get in if there were lights in any event."

With that she pushed past him and passed out into the hall. Hurrying along she ran up the stairs and entered her bed-room. Five minutes later she came down again. Her figure was concealed in a long ulster, heavy boots were on her feet, and a soft slouch hat was pulled well down on her head.

From beneath the ulster peeped the ends of a pair of trousers. For this midnight expedition Yvonne had donned the masculine disguise which had proved so useful to her in the old when she lived but to bring vengeance down upon the eight men who had wrecked the fortunes of her mother and herself in Australia.

Almost simultaneously with her arrival in the hall, there came the sound of a motor outside, and two toots from the horn which told her it was Alec.

Yvonne drew on a pair of gloves, and, patting her pockets as though to satisfy herself that she had forgotten nothing, she called out a goodbye to Graves.

Then the door closed as she passed out, bent on her purpose.

Drawing out a small torch from her pocket, Yvonne pressed the switch, and cast the circle of light upon the sash of the window.
(Chapter 2.)

Yvonne took another step forward; then she paused,
and a cold chill passed down her spine. (*Chapter 2.*)

WHEN Yvonne arrived within a hundred yards of her destination she took down the speaking-tube and ordered Alec to draw up. Emerging, she closed the door, and stepped ahead until she stood beside him.

"Return here in three-quarters of an hour, Alec," she said, in low tones. "This is a quiet street, and there won't be many people about. If anybody should pass, they will only think you are waiting for someone who is making a late call. When you come back, wait half an hour if I am not here. If I have not come by then, wait no longer, but return to the garage."

As she finished speaking, Yvonne turned and strode down the street, with an excellent imitation of a man's walk. Seven months before, when she had first grown suspicious of the doings of Gilbert Jefferson, she had contemplated just such a midnight visit to his house as she was bent on this night.

Then she made a survey of his place by daylight in preparation for her visit, and, owing to that, she was perfectly aware of its general lay out. Perhaps that also had influenced her in her sudden decision to make a visit after hearing Channing's report. Had she not known the disposition of the place she would hardly have risked it.

On turning the first corner, she walked on until she came to the mouth of a narrow lane, which passed along at the rear of the houses facing on the two larger streets parallel with it.

The lane was of the unlighted type by night and unattractive type by day, which serves the purpose of a tradesmen's passage to the different houses.

Up this lane she turned, and kept on until she had counted the eighth house from the corner on the right. Then she paused, and stood listening.

"Not a sound," she murmured. "Now to find out if there are any lights showing."

With an agility which would have been surprising even in one thoroughly accustomed to the kind of clothes she was wearing, Yvonne leaped upwards until her hands caught the top of the fence which separated the lane from the rear yard of the house on the other side.

The fact that her boots made no sound as she squirmed up

indicated that the soles were of rubber.

She reached the top without mishap, and sat balanced there for a few moments glancing cautiously about her.

The heavy rain had now ceased; but a dense drizzle was still falling, curtaining the view with a misty shroud. In the house on her right she could make out a single light in a rear room. Beyond it, and away to the left, she could see absolutely none.

The house before her appeared to be in utter darkness and silence. Satisfied that it was safe to proceed, Yvonne dropped to the turf inside, and made her way cautiously across, until she stood close to the wall of the house.

She moved slowly along beside it until her fingers came in contact with a window. A few moments' examination served to show that it evidently opened into a basement room of some sort.

For a moment she hesitated. Should she risk an entry there, or attempt to force a window from the balcony?

If any of the servants slept in the basement she might well blunder in upon them. On the other hand, if the basement were untenanted, it would be a desirable way of entry. She finally decided in its favour, and with this decision she acted.

Drawing out a small electric torch from her pocket, Yvonne pressed the switch, and cast the circle of light upon the sash of the window. She smiled involuntarily as she saw how it was fastened.

"Why will people use such fastenings?" she murmured. "A child could force that with a sixpenny pocket-knife."

Whether this might be possible or not, it certainly presented no difficulties to Yvonne. Extinguishing the torch, she thrust it back in the pocket of her coat; then she drew out a thin piece of strong steel, and felt along the sash for a moment. It only took a second to slip it up between, and in five more a soft snap came as she succeeded in pressing it back.

After that it was child's play indeed. She returned the strip of steel to her pocket, and then pressed the tips of her fingers up against the sash. A soft squeak followed as it moved a trifle. Again she pressed, and again it feebly protested.

Now she could get her fingers beneath the sash and the sill, and this she proceeded to do. Slowly and steadily she lifted, until the window was open a sufficient height to permit her to squeeze through.

Two minutes later she stood inside, casting the light from the torch about the room, which was undoubtedly an unused laundry. A door in the farther wall stood half open, and, after a further survey of her surroundings, she made towards it. It revealed another and larger room, which she took for the servants' dining-hall.

Off this opened the kitchen, and from that led a flight of stairs to the floor above. So far she had seen no signs that any of the servants slept down there. She reached the stairs in safety, and proceeded to ascend. One or two of the boards creaked loudly under her weight; but, after pausing to listen each time, she kept on.

At the top the torch revealed a passage opening into a butler's pantry. From there she passed into a large dining-room, and from that into another passage to a big lounge hall. The light revealed several doors opening off it, but instinctively Yvonne chose one on the right.

"I'll try this one first," she muttered to herself. "I may be wrong; but, if so, will have to keep on trying until I find the study."

She stole softly forward until she was close to the door. Then she extinguished the electric torch and stood, scarcely breathing. The big house seemed wrapped, almost in utter silence.

From time to time she could hear a creak, or one of those numerous sounds which are a part of the habitation of man in the dark hours of the night. Somewhere up the hall a clock ticked, and, even as she stood by the door, it rattled and wheezed loudly until it finally chimed a sonorous twelve.

"Just midnight," she breathed. "I have made good time so far. Now for the next and most important step."

Drawing a long breath, she softly turned the handle of the door and pushed it gently. It opened inwards without a sound, and as she squeezed through the soft brush of velvet against her face told her a heavy sliding portiere was attached to the inner part of the door.

She clicked her teeth in satisfaction as her hands confirmed this. It would enable her to work by the light of the room, for the heavy curtain would keep any rays from filtering beneath the door.

Closing the door, and releasing the handle as silently as she had turned it, she again brought the torch into requisition.

She was standing now just inside the door, the torch in her right hand, and the fingers of her left straying about on the wall in search of the switch which would turn on the lights. Then the circle of light from the torch fell upon the carpeted floor in front of her.

With her left hand still mechanically feeling for the wall switch, she lifted the torch with the other, and sent its light travelling about the room,

A huge bookcase against the wall to the left told her she had been right in her guess that this was the study. Their titled backs and gilt decorations assumed grotesque shapes in the wavering light, and seemed first to grin at her, then to glower at her like dozens of impish gargoyles.

Passing from that, she saw next a big mantelpiece, with a pile of ashes in the grate beneath. Before it were two big easy chairs. Their positions, and the ashes in the grate, told her that the room had undoubtedly been occupied during the evening.

Then the light revealed a big heavily-draped window. Next, another bookcase, then a window similar to the other, and after that a big mahogany desk. As the light fell upon this Yvonne gave a sigh of satisfaction. That desk was her objective.

At this moment her fingers found the switch on the wall. She turned it, and at once the room was flooded with light, revealing the richness of its furnishings in a way which the torch failed to do.

Yvonne started towards the desk, but she had taken less than three steps when she drew up with a sharp intake of breath. Not until that moment had she seen something which hung over the side of the big high-backed desk-chair.

That something was a human arm, and, being what it was, it meant in the natural course of events that a human body must be concealed behind the high back of the chair.

Was it Jefferson? And if so, had he fallen asleep before the desk? If he had, it was strange that the sudden turning on of the light had not awakened him.

Yvonne took another step forward; then she paused, and a cold chill passed down her spine.

For the first time she had seen a dark stain on the carpet at the bottom of the chair. It was a silent suggestion of a sinister nature. Yet Yvonne was no coward, and, since she had gone so far, she was determined to go still further.

Another, step and another step —she took, until she could now see a shoulder and part of a crumpled-up body. Another step, and the thing in the chair was in full view. It was the body of a man hunched up in the chair, with his hands hanging loosely and his head sunk on his chest. Only the edge of the desk kept him from slipping forward to

15

the floor.

With a shudder, Yvonne drew nearer and yet nearer. On the floor, directly beneath the right hand, was a pen, and on the blotting-pad a letter.

Turning away from the figure in the chair, Yvonne bent forward and, scanned the written lines.

It was dated that day, and was unfinished, mute evidence to the curious that the writer had been struck down even as he wrote.

It was begun:

"My dear Niece," and went on to say that the writer would be pleased to have the niece arrange to come and visit him for a few weeks. He next mentioned that he was getting a motor, and was evidently beginning to say how the niece would "enjoy" it, when at the word "enjoy" his fate had overtaken him.

The letter "y" broke off in a sharp upward stroke, which continued on in a blotchy line across the paper and towards the edge of the desk, showing how the pen had fallen and rolled to the floor when the writer had been struck down.

With another shiver, Yvonne bent to scan the face of the man who had been murdered, and whom she was now positive was none other than Gilbert Jefferson himself. But her intention was halted almost ere she had put it into effect, and she sank back against the desk, struggling with all her strength to keep from shrieking aloud at the awful thing she had seen.

And well she might, for not only had the murderer taken the life of his victim; but, in a fit of what was evidently a fiendish rage, he had so disfigured the dead man's face with some terrible acid as to make it absolutely unrecognisable.

It was a fearful sight, and now all thought of her own purpose in coming gone from her mind, Yvonne moved towards the door shudderingly.

Then her already taut nerves threatened to give way entirely as, half-way across the room, she was brought up by the sound of a terrific ringing of bells. They seemed to be literally all over the house. Following this came a loud pounding on the front door. Then the ringing sounded again, then the pounding. Someone was at the door, determined to enter the house without delay. What did it mean?

Like a flash it broke over Yvonne what her position would be did anyone enter and discover her there in the room with the murdered man. Her burglarious entry, her masculine disguise, her electric torch, her revolver—everything about her would shriek with suggestion.

No amount of explanation could clear away such a mass of circumstantial evidence. She knew that, and knew it would be necessary to act at once were she to get away safely.

Already she could hear the sound of footsteps overhead, and the renewed pounding on the door and ringing of the bell told her it would be but a moment before the door would be opened.

Like a frightened deer she sped to the wall switch by the door and turned off the light. At that moment voices outside told her some of the servants at least had reached the lower hall.

To go out by the door, and retreat by the way she had entered was now out of the question. The servants outside in the hall forbade that. Only one way gave any promise of success, and, if it proved unduly difficult, it seemed that she must be caught. She had no idea of the reason for the sudden commotion at the front door, but something told her it had to do with the awful thing she had discovered. She did not know why she thought this, but something told her intuitively that it was so.

Even as she raced across the room towards one of the windows she heard the front door open, followed by the heavy tramp of feet and the sound of men's voices. Tearing the window curtains apart, she pressed the switch of the torch, and breathed a sigh of relief as she saw the window catch was a duplicate of the one on the basement window.

In a second she had turned it back and, reckless now of any noise she might make, lifted the sash. At that same moment she heard the handle of the door behind her turn, and felt the sudden sweep of the curtains as the draught caught them.

Then, placing one hand on the sill, she hopped over, praying that she might land safely. Not half her figure had cleared the sill before the room behind her was flooded with light. A babel of shouts followed, and just as she landed safely on the turf outside she heard a shrill whistle directly over her head.

Now she knew who the men were who had entered —the police. Something had brought them on the scene, yet, even as she raced for the rear fence, Yvonne wondered how they could have known of the murder, or expected to find anything when the whole household itself had slept in ignorance.

But she had scant time for such thoughts as these. All her mind, all her energies, all her wit was needed for the task in hand. A distant whistle, then another and another, told her the one from the window had been heard, and that soon reinforcements of police would be upon the scene.

Already lights were going up in the adjoining houses, and more than one window was being pushed up. The sounds of pursuit behind her were growing nearer and nearer. One of the men at least had followed her over the sill.

As she realised this she redoubled her efforts to reach the rear fence. A servant in an upstairs window of the house on her left saw her flying figure, and shouted hysterically. Still she kept on, and, with a wave of relief, felt the fence. Leaping it with more speed than dignity, she scrambled over.

Once in the lane outside she sped along as fast as she could. She knew, only too well, how soon the police would have its exits guarded. She reached the end in safety, and, looking back as she turned into the larger street, could see a figure lumbering along after her.

Now she began to pray devoutly that nothing had detained Alec. If he had followed her instructions to the letter, he must be waiting. If not —well, she must still trust to her own ingenuity.

She tore along until she reached the corner, then she swung into the other street. Her heart gave a great leap as she saw the limousine drawn up at the kerb a little way down, though the vision of another policeman coming along this street at top speed told her it would be touch and go with her.

As she ran she whistled a shrill signal to Alec, every moment was precious now, and if he were ready to dash off at once as soon as she readied him she might yet get clear. Nor did he fail her.

As she drew closer and closer the car began to move very slowly, then she put on a last desperate spurt and tumbled head-long into the front beside him just as he sent the car ahead with a jerk.

A moment later it had gathered greater speed, and Yvonne knew that for the time, at least, she was safe. The sound of the police whistles still followed them, but she knew that, with a fair start, Alec was clever enough to throw off pursuit.

She lay some minutes getting back her breath, then, scrambling up, she sat down in the driver's seat beside Alec.

"Double and redouble on your tracks!" she gasped, "The pursuit will be keen, and we simply must shake it off."

Alec's nod told her she could depend on him to do everything that was possible, and she leaned back, letting the wind play on her pounding temples. Slowly her mind was going back to what she had just seen.

Then from that it jumped to the fruitless result of her own visit there. A moment later she was sitting up rigid, with her heart pounding as it had not pounded even when she leaped over the sill. For she had just remembered something.

Graves, her uncle, had begged of her not to go to Gilbert Jefferson's house that night. He had turned ashen when she had even mentioned Jefferson's name, and his agitation had been very strange indeed. It were almost as though he had known what she must find there.

And now she also remembered the promise he had exacted should she see lights in the house or any signs of a commotion about it. Commotion was the word he had used, and it was a strangely-fitting one for what had actually happened after her arrival. What — oh, what did it mean?

And even as she asked herself the question a great weight descended upon Yvonne's heart.

DETECTIVE-INSPECTOR THOMAS, of Scotland Yard, was a very worried man. There was no shrewder or more competent trailer of criminals at the Yard than he, nor had any man a finer record. Yet he was worried —and with reason. For some months now he had been in a similar state of mind.

Beginning with the strange disappearance of Major Philip Goode six months before, and continuing until the present, there had occurred several crimes through the country which called for elucidation, and the arrest of the different perpetrators, neither of which had been accomplished so far.

As the pick of the Yard, Inspector Thomas had been assigned to special service on the matter four months before. That was at the time of the disappearance of Dr. Finn, the well-known scientist, as he was crossing the Channel from Folkestone to Boulogne.

His investigations up to the month following had proved abortive, when suddenly another crime occurred —the cold-blooded murder of Mr. Herbert Welkin, M.P., as he was walking home from his club one night. It was then that Inspector Thomas had sought his old friend, Sexton Blake.

With his usual willingness to contribute of his best to the cause of law and order, Blake had done all he could to assist the inspector, but even his keen mind had failed to grasp any clue which led to anything tangible.

Almost every form of theory imaginable had been fitted to the problem.

Every crime for years past had been looked up and carefully studied. The different unsolved disappearances and murders had been treated as the work of separate and distinct criminals; now they were treated as the work of one hand and as the work of a gang.

The whereabouts of every known and suspected criminal, both in England and on the Continent, was investigated. The Continental, as well as the New York, police lent every aid in their power. Individuals were arrested on suspicion, and a case built up against them, only to collapse in the face of an undoubted alibi.

In fact, every resource known to a resourceful Yard had been brought into play, with their cleverest man to handle the work. Yet not a single gleam of light appeared. And now the Commissioner of

Police was getting impatient.

Inspector Thomas, as the man in charge of the investigations, was the recipient of this impatience, and, in his worry, he had again sought Sexton Blake. Not that he, or anyone at the Yard, minded the yapping of the papers; they were used to that by now.

What he did mind was the fact that for once everything they said was true, and he began to realise that, unless he made some headway soon he was slated for retirement. And Detective inspector Thomas had a wife and children to look after, just the same as lots of other men whose feelings and affections were not compressed behind blue-uniformed officialdom.

Blake himself, though not as interested in the solution of the problem as the Yard was, felt irritated that so far their combined work had come to naught. He had an uncomfortable feeling that somewhere in the world, and probably not far from London itself, there was somebody chuckling over the discomfiture of the police.

It seemed an extraordinary thing that, whether the crimes were each due to a separate and distinct hand, or whether they emanated from the one source, not the slightest clue could be found.

As it was a miserable night outside, and a cosy one within, Blake was not averse to the inspector's company, particularly as his own work was well up to time, and that marvel of precision and neatness, Tinker, had made all entries in the Index up to that very day itself. At present he was doing something in the laboratory, with Pedro as company.

Blake and the inspector sat before the fire in the consulting-room. They had been sitting thus for two hours, discussing, in low tones, the cases which puzzled the man from Scotland Yard from every point of view.

To the inspector's plain recital of all the evidence he had gathered Blake had been adding his own analytical suggestions, and yet, so far, they had wound up in the inevitable impasse each time.

It was just half-past eleven when the desk 'phone rang violently. With a word of apology to the inspector, Blake rose, and, crossing to the desk, lifted the receiver.

"Hallo! Hallo!" he called. "What? Who is speaking? Oh, yes! All right. The inspector is here. One moment. I will call him."

He turned and signed to his guest.

"Someone at the Yard wants to speak to you. Says it is urgent."

The inspector rose with alacrity.

"Thanks. I will speak with them."

A moment later his deep tones rang out.

"Hallo! Yes, this is Inspector Thomas speaking. Oh, it is you, Gordon! What is the trouble? What? A strange message you say? Read it. Wait a minute until I get pencil and paper."

Blake, who had anticipated his request, thrust the required articles beneath his hand, then returned to his seat by the fire.

"All right!" called the inspector. "Go ahead!"

For some moments he wrote steadily as the voice at the other end of the wire repeated some message to him. Then he stopped writing, and began to speak again.

"Tell Sergeant Mullin to take three men and leave for Fulton Terrace at once. I shall go on from here, and should be there about the same time they arrive. Tell the sergeant to lose no time. This thing may be a hoax. I am inclined to think it is. At the same time, we mustn't ignore it. That is all. Good-bye!"

As he hung up the receiver he tore from the pad the sheet of paper on which he had been writing, and handed it to Blake.

"Read that, Blake," he said, "and tell me what you think of it."

"I can tell what you think of it," smiled Blake, as he took it. "I heard you say you thought it was a hoax."

Lifting the sheet of paper, he read what was written. It was evidently the copy of a message which had been repeated over the 'phone, and read as follows:

"Scotland Yard. Come to No. 12A, Fulton Terrace on the receipt of this. Urgent."

It was unsigned. The inspector had also received the memoranda showing the details of its delivery at the Yard. It had been handed to a lad in Knightsbridge about a quarter to eleven, with instructions to take it to the Yard at once. The man who had given it to the lad had also given him a sovereign, telling him to take a taxi, and keep the change.

Then the man had hurried away, and the boy, desiring to retain as much of the money as possible, had made the journey by 'bus and on foot. That accounted for its tardy delivery.

When he had finished reading all there was to read Blake handed it back.

"Rather brief and mysterious, to say the least," he said. "It may be a hoax, as you say, but it is rather an expensive one. It is only fools or knaves who prowl around at night throwing away sovereigns for the sake of a practical joke. I heard you give orders for a sergeant and three men to proceed there at once. That means, I suppose, that you are not thoroughly convinced of its humorous intent?"

The inspector nodded.

"When I called it a hoax I was forgetting about the sovereign," he said. "Still, joke or no joke, we don't dare disregard it. They may have the laugh on us, but if we didn't go, they might have a bigger laugh. I don't suppose you care to come?"

"On the contrary, inspector, I am rather keen to go with you. My curiosity is aroused. I am anxious to see why the police should be so strangely summoned to No. 12A, Fulton Terrace, at this time of night. By the way, that is rather a quiet and aristocratic residential street, isn't it?"

"Yes. It is mostly given up to wealthy merchants and stockbrokers. I shall be pleased to have you come along. If you are ready, we will waste no time. Perhaps we can pick up a taxi outside."

"We will get one all right," remarked Blake, as he turned to enter the dressing-room.

He called out to Tinker as he emerged, wearing a soft hat and long raincoat. When the lad appeared, he told him where he was going; then, after assisting the inspector into his things, they passed out together.

Luck was with them in the form of a crawling taxi which was coming down on the opposite side of the street. Blake whistled to it, and as it drew into the kerb he gave the address. Then he entered after the inspector.

"Ugh!" grunted the latter, as the door closed. "It is a beastly night."

"I must say the warmth of an open fire is far more desirable than this driving mist," replied Blake; "but perhaps we shall find enough of interest at our destination to repay us for the discomfort of the journey."

Little he dreamed how prophetic his casually uttered words were to prove.

Whatever doubts either of them may have had as to the serious nature of the message were dispelled as soon as the taxi turned into Fulton Terrace. It was obvious that something very much out of the usual was taking place.

The usually quiet —and at night deserted —street was buzzing with people and excitement. Lights shone from several of the houses, and, a little way down, before one of them, was collected quite a little crowd.

As their taxi reached there, Blake and the inspector could see that it was composed of people in all stages of undress— evidence that something had occurred to rouse them from their beds and bring them out to satisfy their curiosity.

As they descended, and pushed their way through, they heard more than once the word "Murder" coupled with the name of Gilbert Jefferson, together with a few disjointed details regarding the man who had evidently been the victim.

Looking up at the fan-light over the door, Blake read the number 12A illuminated by the light inside. So, after all, the message had been no hoax.

Two policemen were already on guard at the door keeping back the crowd, but as soon as they recognised Inspector Thomas they moved aside, permitting him and Blake to enter.

Inside they found five servants standing in a huddled group in the hall, while from a room at the far end came the sound of deep voices. Towards this the newcomers strode.

Pushing open the door, the inspector entered, with Blake close behind him. A single glance told them that the word they had heard outside had been no idle rumour.

Sergeant Mullin was there with two constables. He was in the act of making laborious notes when Blake and the inspector appeared, but as he recognised his superior he saluted, and made a gesture towards the high-backed chair in front of the desk.

"The message was no joke, sir," he said, "Murder —brutal murder."

"Any clue?" asked the inspector sharply,

"A simple case, sir; but, unfortunately, we just missed catching the murderer."

"Tell me what you know."

"We left the Yard at exactly ten minutes to twelve, sir," said the sergeant. "We arrived here at eleven minutes past midnight. The street was silent and deserted. Everything appeared perfectly normal, and I began to think a joke had been played on us. However, we walked on until we reached this place, and rang and pounded alternately until I woke one of the servants.

"Finally we were admitted, and I asked who lived here. The butler said Mr. Gilbert Jefferson was the tenant. I asked if he were at home, and was told he was in bed. Just then I heard a sound in this room at the end of the hall. I ordered my men to follow, and hurried towards the door.

"As I opened it I caught sight of a man's figure just disappearing through that window to the left. I turned on the lights and took after him. At the window I stopped long enough to blow my whistle, then I jumped out.

"He was already making for the fence at the rear, and it was owing to that obstacle that I missed him. He was over it like a shot, and well up the lane before I had been able to get over it. I followed, however, and heard police-whistles in the next street. Then I was confident we should get him.

"As I reached the street at the end of the lane, however, I saw we might lose him, after all. A little way down was a big motor which had evidently been waiting for him. Anyway, he jumped into it, and it drove off at high speed.

"We commandeered a taxi, and took after it, but it gave us the slip. I am sorry, sir, but we did our best. There is no doubt but that he was the man who did the job."

The inspector had listened glumly to the sergeant's recital, but when the latter had finished he made no attempt to rebuke him. Instead, he continued his questioning.

"How was entry gained to the house?"

"By the basement window. We have traced footprints from the rear fence straight up to it. Besides, it was wide open, and the catch showed signs of having been forced."

"Have you made an examination of the body yet?"

"Only a very brief one, sir. I was waiting for you to arrive. He was stabbed from behind, sir, although the murderer withdrew the knife and took it away with him. The blade was thrust straight down above the collar-bone until it pierced the heart. That was the cause of death; but, in addition to that, the murderer committed a fiendish outrage."

"What was it?"

Even the sergeant, accustomed as he was to terrible sights,

shuddered a trifle.

"Will you look for yourself, sir?"

All this time Blake had been standing near, listening in silence to the sergeant's story. He had followed each point carefully, and now, as the inspector crossed to the desk, he went, too. It was evident at a single glance what the sergeant meant by a terrible outrage.

The face of the murdered man had been burned beyond recognition by some powerful acid, and a second glance showed that the hands had suffered the same fate. Simultaneously, the inspector and Blake bent over the desk, and read the half-finished letter which still lay on the blotting-pad.

"Murdered in the very act of writing to his niece," muttered Inspector Thomas, as he straightened up, and sent his gaze roving about the articles on the top of the desk.

Blake said nothing. He gave a brief glance at the pen on the floor which the sergeant now pointed out, and upon which the inspector pounced with avidity.

"We must have a doctor at once," he said, as he laid it down.

"I sent for one, sir," replied the sergeant. "One lives in this street, and he should be here at any moment."

Barely had he finished speaking when the door opened to admit a short, bearded man, wearing glasses, and carrying a small black bag.

"I am Dr. Musgrave," he said, addressing the inspector.

The latter nodded, and pointed to the body in the chair.

"Better make an examination at once, doctor. I suppose you will want him laid on the couch."

"If you please."

The two constables lifted the body gently, and carried it over to the broad leather couch which stood by the wall to the right. Blake and the inspector watched the examination in silence. In less than ten minutes the doctor looked up.

"Dead," he said briefly. "For less than two hours, I should judge. His body is still warm. I can do nothing."

"All right," said the inspector, "I shall notify the coroner at once."

When the doctor had departed, Inspector Thomas knelt and began a thorough search of the dead man's pockets. As he brought each article to light he handed it to the sergeant, who in turn laid it on the desk. When the inspector had finished, he beckoned to Blake, and together they bent to examine the little collection.

There was a bunch of keys, a few coppers, three and six in silver, a long leather wallet which had been ripped apart, and contained a portion of what had been a five-pound note, an empty coin purse, a couple of letters addressed to Gilbert Jefferson, Esq., a lead pencil, and two white linen handkerchiefs, each bearing in the corner the initials "G. J." That was all. There was no sign of watch and chain, cigarette or cigar case, or any knick-knacks of any value.

"What do you make of it?" grunted the inspector, turning to Blake.

"Let's have your opinion," countered Blake.

"H'm! I make it cold-blooded, brutal murder, with robbery as the motive. Look at this empty coin purse; see this torn wallet, with only a portion of a note left. The thief overlooked that in his haste. Furthermore, there is no watch and chain —in fact, nothing of any value.

"I noticed also, when the doctor was making his examination, that the dead man's scarf was slightly marked just below the knot, showing he had worn a scarf pin there with one of those safety points on it. It had undoubtedly been torn from it by force.

"And if you look at the little finger of his left hand you will see a mark made by a ring which had been worn there. The acid didn't obliterate that, and the ring isn't there now."

"Your theory certainly seems strongly endorsed by the visible facts," remarked Blake slowly. "But how about examining the servants? Perhaps you can gather some information of value from them."

"That is just what I intend to do now. Sergeant, call in the butler first."

The sergeant moved to the door, and, opening it, beckoned to one of the servants outside. A moment later the butler had entered. He was a middle-aged servitor of the old-fashioned type —bent, sombre, and conscientious.

At present he was obviously greatly affected by the terrible shock he had received, and when his eyes fell upon the figure on the couch he all but collapsed. Blake reached a carafe of brandy from a near-by stand, and pouring some into a glass, with some soda, handed it to the butler.

"Here," he said kindly, "drink this. It will brace you up. Keep your nerve, my man, and don't look towards the couch. We know how this affair must affect you, but the inspector wished to ask you some questions, and you must help him all you can."

"Thank you, sir," replied the butler gratefully, as he gulped down the brandy. "I'm sure, sir, I shall do everything I can to help the police catch the man who has killed my poor master."

"Now, then," broke in the inspector, "if you feel better, give me your attention. Was your master out last evening?"

"Not after he had dinner, sir."

"At what time did you last see him?"

"It was just past ten, sir."

"Did he seem perfectly normal?"

"Well, sir, he was much as he had been for the past few days."

"What do you mean by that?" asked the inspector sharply.

"He hadn't been any too well sir. Nervous and irritable, if I might say so, sir."

"Ah, he had been nervous, eh? Make a note of that, sergeant. Now, then— By the way, what is your name?"

"Parker, sir."

"Very well, Parker. Now tell me all you can about the evening. Be brief."

"The master came home about seven, as usual, sir. He ordered dinner for a quarter to eight. Afterwards he came in here, where he had his coffee. That was a habit of his, sir. Then he sent for Mrs. Hodgkins, the housekeeper, and told her to prepare Miss Alice's room, as he was writing to ask her to come and visit."

"That is the niece, I suppose?"

"Yes, sir. After Mrs. Hodgkins had gone he told me he expected a caller about nine-thirty. He said it was a man who worked for him, and that I was to show him in at once."

"Ah, he had a visitor, did he? Why didn't you say so before? Go on!"

"He arrived at exactly nine-thirty, and I showed him into the study. The master was sitting at the desk."

"What did the caller look like?"

"He was medium height, sir, and looked to me like a man who might work about the docks. He was dressed roughly, and wore no overcoat. The collar of his coat was turned up, and he was very wet."

"How did your master greet him?"

"Friendly like, sir. He said 'Ah, you are on time. Come in!' Then he told me to fix the whisky and glasses, and as I went out I heard him telling his visitor to help himself. I went down to the basement then, sir, to see that everything was fastened for the night.

"With the exception of the cook, the servants had all retired. It was the cook's night out, and just as I started to come upstairs, she came in. We stood talking in the kitchen until ten o'clock. Then the master's bell rang. I started up to answer it, and the cook went to bed. The man who had called was still there, and —"

"Where were they sitting?"

"The master was still at his desk, and his visitor in that chair beside it."

"What was their manner then?"

"Just the same, sir. The master was talking in a friendly way, and the other was laughing at something the master had said. He told me not to wait up any longer, and that he would let his visitor out himself.

"I told him I didn't mind staying up, but he ordered me to go to bed. He added that he might be writing late. I did as he told me, sir, and know nothing more of what happened until I heard the police at the front door."

"You don't know if the other servants saw anything or not?"

"Well, sir, the cook, who did not retire until close on eleven, said she heard the front door close about half-past ten. Her room is on the top floor in the front. She looked out and saw a man walking away.

"She told me this out in the hall a few minutes ago. I asked her what the man looked like. She said he wore a soft black hat and had no overcoat. From her description, I should say it was the man who called on the master."

"She heard no sounds either before or after that?"

"No, sir; nor did any of the other servants."

"You are quite positive as to the time the cook heard the front door close, and saw a man walking away?"

"She seemed so, sir."

"Very well, Parker. That will do. When you go out, send in the cook."

The butler made his way out as though glad to be released. Before the cook came in, Blake drew a large screen in front of the couch, in order that she might not be unnerved and become hysterical.

She was a big, raw-boned woman, with a broad Irish accent, and for all her bulk, seemed completely broken up by the events of the evening. The inspector's questions were very brief.

"What is your name?" he asked curtly.

"Emily O'Connor, sir."

"Parker, the butler, says you heard the front door close this evening after you had gone to your room."

"I did, sir."

"What time was it?"

"Just on half-past ten, sir."

"You looked out of the window?"

"Yes, sir, and saw a man walking away."

"Describe him."

"I couldn't see much, sir. He wore a soft black hat, and a dark suit of some sort. He wore no overcoat, and carried no umbrella, though it was raining hard then. I described him to Parker, who says the man who called on the master was dressed that way, and it must have been him."

"Never mind any theories," said Inspector Thomas curtly. "What time did you go to bed?"

"About eleven."

"You saw or heard nothing out of the ordinary, from the time you saw the man leave the house until you retired?"

"No, sir."

"That will do. You may go."

When the door had closed behind her, the inspector turned to Blake.

"If the man who called on Jefferson left at ten-thirty, he can't be the man who did the murder," he said with a puzzled frown.

"Providing the murder was committed after that hour." replied Blake.

"Well, even supposing it was done before then, and that he did it, we still have the presence of the man whom the sergeant surprised to account for. That was past midnight— over an hour and a half after the other man had departed."

"Might it be possible that the man —" began the sergeant, and then broke off.

"Might what be possible?" snapped the inspector irritably. "Finish what you started to say."

The sergeant flushed.

"I was going to suggest, sir, that the man who had left at half-past ten might have returned later, perhaps to get the knife with which he did the job, but then I remembered that he was without an overcoat, whereas the man I surprised here wore a long one."

"He wouldn't have the nerve, anyway," remarked the inspector. "Well, Blake, you have seen everything and heard everything. Do you agree with my theory?"

"What is that exactly, inspector?"

"That Gilbert Jefferson was murdered, with robbery as the motive, either by the man who was with him during the evening, or by the man who was surprised in the study here by the sergeant."

"I am afraid I do not care to commit myself to an opinion yet," said Blake, "For instance, several alternatives might be the case. The man who visited Jefferson during the evening might have murdered him for some private reason, and made his escape.

"The man who was here when the sergeant entered may have been an ordinary burglar, who just happened to break in on the same night. He may have been as much surprised at the sight of the body as was the sergeant. Also, he may be the one who got away with everything of value on Jefferson's person.

"Again, the man who called during the evening may be entirely innocent of the deed. The man who was here when the sergeant arrived may be responsible for the whole busness.

"Still another theory occurs to me. That is that the man who was here during the evening, and the man whom the sergeant surprised are one and the same. The man who left at ten-thirty may have procured a coat, and returned as the sergeant suggested. He certainly had plenty of time to do so.

"And then again, each and all of these theories may be utterly wrong. Investigation may show an entirely different line to follow. For instance, inspector, let me remind you of something."

"What?"

"The mysterious message which was the cause of bringing us all here to-night."

"By heavens! That had entirely slipped my mind."

"Do you remember what time it was handed to a boy in Knightsbridge to be taken to Scotland Yard?"

"At a quarter to eleven."

"Exactly. And Knightsbridge is just about ten minutes' walk from here. Now recall something else. The cook heard the front door slam, and saw a man walking away at half-past ten.

"That means, supposing he walked to Knightsbridge, he would have just about time enough to reach there and hand the message to a boy at a quarter to eleven. Mind you, I am only suggesting that he may have been the man who did that. Now let us deal with the message itself.

"If you will remember, it said 'Come to No. 12a, Fulton Terrace.' It did not say 'Go to No. 12a, Fulton Terrace.' That tells us one thing. The message was written here in this house, for the writer unconsciously worded it under the influence of his surroundings. If he had written it outside, he would have written 'Go' instead of 'Come.'

"Now that brings us to another theory. We know, it is unusual for a man of Jefferson's standing to be on intimate terms with a man who works about the docks, yet we have the butler's evidence telling us they were. Very well.

"Supposing, for the sake of argument, that Jefferson's visitor brought him news of some danger which threatened, and that Jefferson was afraid it might come upon him that night. What more natural than that he should write a note asking for police protection, and give it to his visitor to send to the Yard as he departed.

"Let us presume he had an idea it might come about midnight, and also presume he was a courageous, self-reliant man. He might refuse to permit his visitor to stay and lend him his aid, but might request him to send the message to the police knowing it would bring them to his aid by midnight at latest.

"This it would have done if the boy to whom the message was given had taken a taxi as he was ordered to do. As it was, the police arrived here just after midnight, and surprised a man in the study. That man might have been the danger which Jefferson thought threatened him.

"We can tell if Jefferson was the writer of the message by comparing it with the letter on the desk. And that leads us to another point.

"Supposing the man who left the house at ten-thirty were the murderer. It isn't likely that he would be instrumental in bringing the police on the scene. Instead, he would do all in his power to prevent discovery until he made a safe getaway.

"Furthermore, supposing he were the man who sent the note to the Yard, then it would be impossible to think he was the same man who was surprised here after midnight by sergeant.

"If he sent the note, he would know what was in it, and would know that to return would be to risk falling into the hands of the police.

"No, inspector, I must say I do not think your theory will hold water. In the first place, in all the records of crime, a burglar invariably commits unpremeditated murder. It is done on the spur of the moment, and, furthermore, nine times out of ten a burglar will run before he will kill.

"Even if Jefferson were killed by a burglar, that would not account for the disfigurement of his face and hands by acid. That breathes very strongly of premeditation, and if that is so, then the torn wallet, the empty coin-purse, the missing ring and scarf-pin were taken as a blind, and to suggest robbery as the motive.

"I am afraid this crime is of far deeper nature than it seems at first blush. It may be on a par with the crimes we were discussing at Baker Street this very evening, and indeed may be part and parcel of the same series.

"Were I to suggest anything, I should say find the man who visited Jefferson during the evening, and find the man who was surprised here by the sergeant. When you have accomplished that, you may be a good step ahead in your investigation."

"You have suggested so many theories and alternatives that my head is whirling with them," muttered the inspector. "As you propounded each one, it seemed a likely one until you went on to another, which shattered the last, and seemed that it must be the one. As a final result you have shattered them all, and suggest that we find two different men."

"I am afraid that is how my arguments appear," smiled Blake, "but they are the outgrowth of what my eyes and mind tell me. I am thoroughly convinced, however, that this murder was premeditated.

"It is too early yet to say more, but I am sure you will find many things before long to prove my contention. If I can be of any assistance at any time in the matter you can count on me."

"Thanks," answered the inspector. "If I wish to consult you I shall take advantage of your offer."

Already his open discursive manner of earlier in the evening had departed, and a stiff formality had taken its place. He was chagrined at the sudden shattering of his hasty theory by Blake, and annoyed at the cascade of other theories and alternatives which the latter had suggested.

He would not have minded so much had they been alone, but in view of the fact that he was still unsuccessful in his search for the perpetrators of several crimes which had occurred, and that his men had seen him practically dazed by the torrent of words which had fallen from Blake's lips, he had become touchy.

Blake, however, knew him too well to take umbrage at his sudden change of attitude. Instead, he smiled tolerantly and turned to the door.

"I think I shall be going now," he said. "I can be of no use at present, and besides, you will wish to work on your own. If you want me at the inquest, let me know."

"All right. It will probably be to-morrow. At any rate, I shall send you word."

With that, Blake took his departure. Under the urgings of the police, the crowd which had been gathered in the street outside had pretty well departed by now, though lights in several of the houses showed that the sensation was still being eagerly discussed.

The taxi in which he and the inspector had arrived was still waiting. He entered it and ordered the man to drive to Baker Street. On his arrival, Blake took out his note-book and seated himself at his desk.

For a solid hour he wrote steadily, making elaborate notes of everything he had seen and heard at No. 12 A, Fulton Terrace that night. Then he retired and slept dreamlessly until a sun splash on his face woke him at eight the following morning.

All the papers had accounts of a more or less elaborate description of the crime. Nearly all of them gave a brief sketch of Gilbert Jefferson and his business, and nearly all of them accepted the inspector's tentative theory that the motive was robbery.

Over the breakfast table Blake detailed all he had seen to Tinker, who had read of the murder in the papers before Blake was up.

At a few minutes before ten the inspector 'phoned up and asked Blake if he could be on hand for the inquest at eleven. Blake signified that he would, so, at a quarter to eleven, he and Tinker took their departure.

The inquest was much the same as any other inquest —morbid

and depressing. The room in which it was held was crowded.

Over to the right of the coroner and his jury were grouped the servants, while in advance of them sat a slender, girlish figure, dressed in black, and with her features heavily veiled.

Blake ascertained from Inspector Thomas that it was Miss Jefferson, the niece to whom the dead man had been writing when he was struck down.

Sergeant Mullin was the first witness. He detailed exactly the same story which he had told the previous night, and, as he reached the part where he had had the exciting chase, a pin could have been heard to drop, so intense was the interest.

Inspector Thomas came next. He told what he had seen, and dealt with the mysterious message which had been received at the Yard, which had been the cause of the police reaching the scene of the crime so soon after its perpetration.

He had brought with him both the message and the half-finished letter which the dead man had evidently been writing when he was struck down. They were handed to the jury, who agreed that there was not the slightest doubt they had been written by the same hand. That seemed to stamp the dead man, therefore, as the sender of the message.

After the inspector, Blake was called. He simply corroborated what the previous witness had said.

Then came Miss Jefferson. She was assisted into the box by the inspector, and when she lifted her veil, she revealed a very lovely face now set with sorrow, and tear-dimmed eyes.

She answered the few questions put to her in low tones, and seemed relieved when it was over. The sum and substance of her evidence was that both the message and the letter found on the desk were unquestionably in her late uncle's handwriting.

Then came the servants. Parker, the butler, confirmed the inspector's theory that a scarf-pin had been torn from the cravat, and a ring had been forced off the finger of the dead man. He stated that his late master had always worn a valuable pearl scarf-pin which had possessed a guard point, and a large solitaire diamond on the little finger of his left hand.

The cook repeated what she had told the previous night, and after that Dr. Musgrave gave his evidence. He stated in effect that death had been instantaneous, and was due to a knife stab which had passed downward between the collar-bone and shoulder blades, until it had pierced the heart.

He was not prepared to state exactly how long the murdered man had been dead when he arrived, but gave it as his opinion that death had taken place within the preceding two hours. In answer to a question, he replied that it was possible the murder might have been committed between ten and ten-thirty o'clock.

After one or two unimportant witnesses had been called, the question was submitted to the jury. The verdict was exactly what had been expected by everybody.

The late Gilbert Jefferson had been murdered by some person or persons unknown, and an addition was made expressing sympathy with his niece. Then the proceedings closed, and the inquest broke up.

As he passed out, Blake took the inspector's arm.

"Any news yet of the two men for whom you are searching?"

"Not a bit," answered the other. "But I have the drag net out as well as every loophole of escape blocked up. I'll run them to earth or leave the Force," he added viciously.

"I hope you succeed in getting them," said Blake.

With that he joined Tinker, and they returned at once to Baker Street for lunch.

They had hardly finished when the 'phone in the consulting-room rang, and Tinker, who had gone to answer it returned to say that Blake was wanted.

He rose at once and passed out.

"Hello!" he said.

"Hello!" came the voice from the other end. "Is that Mr. Sexton Blake?"

"Yes."

"Can you arrange to come round to No. 12A, Fulton Terrace this afternoon, about half-past two, Mr. Blake?"

"Who is speaking, and why am I wanted?"

"This is Formby Mott speaking. I am solicitor to the estate of the late Gilbert Jefferson. Miss Jefferson saw you at the inquest this morning, and is most anxious to consult with you. Can I tell her you will be here?"

"Yes," responded Blake. "You can expect me at No. 12A, Fulton Terrace at two-thirty sharp."

While the butler stood watching his operations, with puzzlement and not a little awe, Blake began to make his measurements.

(*Chapter 4*).

**After a cursory glance at the papers which littered the desk, Blake drew out his pocket-glass and examined the locks of the drawers.**
*(Chapter 4.)*

## The Fourth Chapter.    £20,000 in Gold Missing —The Ebony Skulls.

SEXTON BLAKE'S friends had a habit of saying that the great detective was in league with the powers who took it upon themselves to regulate that mysterious and world-powerful thing known as "Greenwich time."

This amiable criticism of Blake arose from his almost uncanny faculty for being neither before, nor behind, the time he had set for any appointment. It seemed, sometimes, as though he could foresee such things as traffic blocks, and all the dozen occurrences of a great city which go toward delaying man, particularly when his mission is urgent.

At any rate, it was no idle saying that Blake's name was synonymous with punctuality. Nor did he belie his reputation when, he left Baker Street, bound for No. 12A, Fulton Terrace. A traffic jam in Oxford Circus, another in Piccadilly, a few minutes' pause in order to speak to a passing friend, another stoppage of the taxi in order that he might procure the last editions of the papers, and still, when he rang the bell at the house in Fulton Terrace, it was exactly thirty minutes after two.

At once he was ushered into the library, where such eventful happenings had taken place the night before. Sitting before the desk where the body of the dead man had been found, was a keen-looking young man, garbed in an immaculate grey lounge suit.

Before him was a mass of papers and documents which he had evidently been scrutinising, and on the floor by his feet, a small green solicitor's bag. He rose at once as Blake entered and held out his hand.

"Mr. Blake?" he said interrogatively.

Blake bowed and took the hand held out to him.

"Yes. Mr. Formby Mott, I presume?"

"Exactly. Won't you sit down, Mr. Blake? I will tell you briefly why Miss Jefferson wished me to send for you, then, if you wish, you can question her."

"Perhaps that would be the best idea. Proceed, please."

The lawyer resumed his seat before the desk and cleared his throat.

"Since you were here last night almost as soon as the body of Mr.

Jefferson was discovered, it will be unnecessary for me to touch on that unfortunate part of the affair, Mr. Blake. I did most, if not all, of the late Mr. Jefferson's legal work, so, as soon as I read of the —er— murder in the papers, I wired for his niece. I may say that I drew up Mr. Jefferson's will not long ago, and it was after the discussion of its terms with Miss Jefferson that she wished you sent for.

"To begin with, the will was brief. Mr. Jefferson was worth about sixty thousand pounds in shares of the Jefferson Silk Company, and another twenty thousand pounds in his insurance, made out in two policies of ten thousand each —one policy dated two years ago, and payable to the Jefferson Silk Company, the other dated seven months ago, and made payable to one of the legatees of the will. The will itself disposed of his estate in this manner:

"Half his interest in the Jefferson Silk Company, or roughly thirty thousand pounds in shares, was left to his niece; the policy for ten thousand was left to the company, and, naturally, she would share pro rata in that; this house and its furnishings were also left to his niece; a few bequests were made to the servants, and the balance of the estate, amounting to thirty thousand pounds in shares in the Jefferson Silk Company, together with the second insurance policy of ten thousand, or roughly forty thousand pounds in all, was left to Mr. Hammerton Palmer, the financier.

"Now, on that point, I should like to say something. When Mr. Jefferson came to me some months ago and made his will, he instructed me to state in it that he left this sum to Mr. Palmer for value received during his lifetime. I have an idea that Mr. Jefferson was in financial difficulties at the time, and think it probable that Hammerton Palmer assisted him.

"I went this morning to the offices of the Jefferson Silk Company and, as one of the executors of the will, went through the papers in the safe. There I found the two insurance policies, the will, and several other papers. One of these latter was of some importance. It was no less than a memorandum, made the very day before his death, regarding a sum of twenty thousand pounds in cash which he had drawn against the firm's funds that day. When I saw that, I examined the firm's cheque book and discovered he had drawn the cheque for the amount in the ordinary way.

"Now I come to a peculiar thing about that twenty thousand pounds. In the first place, after the memorandum had dealt with the amount drawn, it contained the following words in his handwriting:

" 'Charge personal account with twenty thousand pounds. In event of my death before repayment, to be repaid by life policy for ten thousand pounds, already made payable to Company and ten thousand pounds in shares to be taken from those left in my will to my niece. None of money or shares left to Hammerton Palmer to be touched.'

"In the second place every penny of the money was drawn in gold. Think of it! Twenty thousand pounds in gold. In itself such a sum drawn in cash is not unusual, but it is unusual to draw it all in gold. I read of the theory of the police that robbery was the motive of the murder, robbery of whatever money and trinkets Mr. Jefferson had on him at the time.

"But, Mr. Blake, that theory was arrived at by the police without any knowledge of the twenty thousand pounds in gold which he drew from the bank. Therefore, in my opinion, the theory of robbery being the motive is strongly endorsed by that fact. And I will now tell you why.

"From the moment I discovered the memorandum in the safe; I have been on the track of that twenty thousand pounds. I went to the bank. It was there I was told how Mr. Jefferson had drawn the money. He telephoned to the bank in the morning and told them he wished that sum in gold. Then he sent a clerk to the bank with the cheque, and at half past two in the afternoon; he himself went there in a taxi.

"The money was handed to him in twenty canvas bags containing one thousand sovereigns each. With the assistance of a clerk from the bank he piled these in the cab and then it drove off. I questioned the clerk on the matter, and he says he heard Mr. Jefferson tell the man to drive to Piccadilly Circus. That is all he knew.

"Well, to make the facts as brief as possible, Mr. Blake, I may say that I have used every effort to trace that twenty thousand pounds but have failed utterly to do so. It has vanished from the assets of the estate as completely and thoroughly as if it had been heaved into the Thames.

"The Silk Company is in ignorance as to the purpose it was used for none of the brokers with whom Mr. Jefferson was in the habit of doing business received it. In fact, they all say that they have had no transactions with Mr. Jefferson for some months. I repeat —it has vanished completely.

"To proceed, Mr. Jefferson's personal account at the Jefferson

Silk Company had a credit of three thousand pounds. If we deduct this from the twenty thousand which he drew in gold, we find that his account now is overdrawn to the tune of seventeen thousand pounds.

"By the terms of his will, the shares and insurance left to Hammerton Palmer must not be touched, and, as seventeen thousand must be repaid to the Silk Company, then that sum will have to be deducted from the shares due to his niece.

Her share of the insurance policy for ten thousand pounds made payable to the Company, will be about six thousand. Add that to the thirty thousand in shares left to her, and we find her total legacy equal to thirty-six thousand pounds. From that is to be deducted the seventeen thousand overdraft, leaving her in possession of nineteen thousand pounds, in addition to the house and furniture."

"In other words her legacy equals, roughly, the sum drawn by Gilbert Jefferson in cash," interrupted Blake, who had sat listening to the lawyer with the closest attention.

"Exactly. In fact, to put the thing in a nutshell, it stands roughly, this way. The full estate amounts to eighty thousand pounds. Hammerton Palmer, the financier, receives roughly forty thousand, or half the estate; Miss Jefferson receives roughly twenty thousand, or a quarter of the estate, and the other quarter has disappeared in the form of twenty thousand pounds in gold.

"Now I come to Miss Jefferson herself. As soon as she got my wire she came on at once. In fact she was at the inquest. Immediately afterwards I went into matters with her and told her how she stood. Of course, we may recover the missing twenty thousand, but that is, naturally, uncertain.

"When she had grasped how matters stood she insisted upon sending for you. She agrees with the police theory that her uncle was murdered and robbed, and, with me, thinks the twenty thousand pounds in gold was the motive. She is determined to track the murderers down and bring them to justice, even if it costs every penny her uncle left her.

"That is why she sent for you, Mr. Blake, and, as executor of the will, I must say I am inclined to side with her in her attitude. She feels it her duty to devote the money to this purpose before spending a penny for any other purpose, and, knowing her as I do, I am sure she will stick to her decision. Now if you wish I can send for her."

"One moment, Mr. Mott. I should like to ask you a few questions before she comes —questions I cannot ask her. As you remarked when I first arrived, I was here last night shortly after the discovery of the murder, and am in possession of some knowledge at first hand.

"Of course, I was not here in an official capacity, and, naturally, did not make a detailed examination of the body or the room. At the same time, I had a pretty thorough look round so we need not discuss that point in detail. What I wish to ask is this. Have you made a thorough search of his desk here?"

"Yes."

"You discovered no signs of any of the drawers being forced?"

"No."

"H'm. I know we discovered his keys on him last night, and I presume the desk key was amongst them?"

"Yes. It was there, I know."

"The murderer, if he did search the desk for the twenty thousand —always presuming it was there, and that robbery was the motive for the crime, Mr. Mott —he could have used Jefferson's own keys and replaced them in the dead man's pocket when he had finished. I think, if you don't mind, I should like to make a further examination of the desk and room; then, perhaps, we will call Miss Jefferson."

"That means then that you will take the case, Mr. Blake?"

"I think you may count on me to do so."

As he spoke, Blake rose and crossed to the desk. He gave a cursory glance at the papers which littered the top, then he drew out his pocket glass. Though to all appearance he now became totally engrossed in the task of examining the lock of each drawer, his mind was really running on what he had seen the night before, and the maze of theories he had propounded to Inspector Thomas.

Those he had voiced, more to prove to the inspector how easy it was to pick holes in the police theory than for any other purpose; but now that he himself was acting officially in the matter, he began to consider them point by point, and search amongst them for one which would contain the gleam of truth which he now sought.

Mechanically he went over every lock as his mind harked back. He reconstructed, mentally, the appearance of the room as it had been when he and the inspector arrived the night before. He once again pictured the body as it had been huddled in the desk-chair. He saw the arm hanging limp; the pen on the floor; the half-written note with the irregular, blurred line across showing how the pen had rolled and fallen.

He saw the note itself which at the inquest Miss Jefferson had identified as in her uncle's writing; he saw the face and hands disfigured by a strong acid. Then his mind went to the strange visitor who had looked like a dock-labourer, and who had spent the evening with the murdered man.

He considered the evidence of the butler, and remembered what the cook had said about a man, dressed as the butler had said his master's visitor was dressed, leaving the house at half past ten.

He gave more than a little thought to the strange and mysterious note received at Scotland Yard a little after eleven, and which had been handed to a boy in Knightsbridge about a quarter to the hour.

At this point Blake made a mental memorandum to find that boy, and get from him a description of the man who had given him the note. Then his mind seized upon the other man who had been in the room that same night —the man who had been surprised by the sergeant and his men at midnight, and who had made good his escape.

The dead man had been murdered between ten and twelve, therefore, both the men who had visited the house that night— one-publicly and the other surreptitiously —must be considered as the possible murderer.

He thought over the possibility of their being one and the same person, but, once more harking back to his theories of the previous night, he felt this to be an improbability. Still, it was within the bounds of possibility and must be treated as such. He arrived at this conclusion and finished his examination of the desk at one and the same moment. Then he returned to his seat.

"I am satisfied that if the twenty thousand pounds in gold was in the desk, none of the drawers were forced in order to obtain it, Mr. Mott," he said. "The locks show no signs of having been tampered with. If the money was there, and it was the motive for the crime, then the man who took it from the desk used Gilbert Jefferson's keys in order to get at it.

"More than that I do not care to say at present. Now if you will call Miss Jefferson I will have a few words with her, although at present I have practically no questions to ask her. Afterwards I should like to make an examination at the back."

"Certainly, Mr. Blake. I will call Miss Jefferson, and I know she will do all in her power to assist you,"

Blake sat in silence while the lawyer crossed to the bell and rang. When the butler appeared he told him to request Miss Jefferson to come down, and a few moments later she came. She was obviously still greatly upset over the tragic occurrence, and greeted Blake in low tones. He put her at her ease at once with a few well-chosen words; then he said:

"I understand from Mr. Mott that you wish me to investigate this sad affair, Miss Jefferson."

She bowed her assent.

"I have just been telling him that I am prepared to do so," went on Blake. "I may wish to consult you from time to time, in order to gain any facts you may know about your late uncle's affairs, but not at present. In the first place I have not completed a preliminary examination, and, in the second place, I have not settled upon a theory for the crime."

"Then you do not agree with the police theory?" she asked quickly.

"I neither agree nor disagree with it," said Blake quietly. "A definite theory is impossible at present, though I must say, the theory of robbery seems more strongly probable than ever, since Mr. Mott has told me of the large sum of money which is missing from the estate.

"Just one other thing, Miss Jefferson, and then I shall detain you no longer. Will you let me impress upon you most strongly the fact that I wish my connection with this affair kept as quiet as possible. I desire to pursue my investigations unhampered, and, I am sure, both you and Mr. Mott will see how essential that is."

"You can depend on me to say nothing, Mr. Blake."

"And on me," put in Mott.

"Then that is all, Miss Jefferson. I will not keep you any longer now. I know how you feel, and I promise you I shall relieve your suspense just as quickly as possible."

"Then you think you can track down the fiend who killed my poor uncle?" cried the girl, the tears starting to her eyes.

"I wish I could assure you of ultimate success," answered Blake soothingly. "But be sure everything possible will be done, and don't forget the police are using every endeavour in the matter."

When she was gone Blake turned to the lawyer.

"I shall now make an examination of the rear of the premises, Mr.

Mott. As you will probably wish to go ahead with your examination of the papers, I shall not ask you to come with me. But I shall be obliged if you will ring for the butler again. He can show me where the entry was made by the man who was surprised by Sergeant Mullin."

The lawyer nodded and crossed to the bell. Almost at once the butler appeared, and in response to the lawyer's instructions, bowed and stood waiting for Blake. The latter, with a last keen look about the library, rose and followed him.

They passed through several rooms and passages to the rear of the house until they came to the stairs leading to the basement. Down these they descended, and kept on until they reached the disused room into which Yvonne had first entered the night before. There Blake drew out his pocket glass and moved at once to the window.

He had little difficulty in discovering the tiny marks on the catch, which showed where it had been forced back. Then he hoisted himself over the sill, and dropped carefully to the ground, Since the ground had been sodden from the heavy rain of the previous evening, each footstep of Yvonne's had left a remarkably clear imprint.

Blake's first procedure was to draw from his pocket his collapsible mould, and arrange it to take an impression of one of the clearest of the prints. This he laid carefully aside, and next drew out his graduated rule. While the butler stood watching his operations, with puzzlement and not a little awe, Blake began to make his measurements.

He measured the imprint first from toe to heel, next across the widest part of the toe, next across the heel, and then across the instep. That done he jotted down the measurements he had taken, and gave his attention to the next imprint. A cursory examination showed this to be undoubtedly made by the same foot, and, from that on, it was easy to follow the trail to the rear wall.

Before rising, however, Blake drew out his measure again and measured the distance between each footprint. Then, proceeding in this fashion, he followed them on to the wall. When he reached the wall he leaned against it and consulted the measurements he had taken.

Though they naturally varied to some extent, he discovered that they were remarkably similar, and a few moments' figuring served to give him the average length of the stride. From the wall Blake moved across until he stood beneath the library window.

Several footprints there almost obliterated those he sought, but after a careful examination it was not difficult for him to see where the man who had been surprised by the sergeant had landed when he jumped through the window, and to trace the rest of his footprints made as he ran for the wall.

Naturally, they were not clear imprints like those made from the wall to the basement windows. Where the latter were made by a slow walking stride the former were made while the owner was running, and only the toe had left an impression.

Blake measured the length between each pair, and, when he had finished, he had as exhaustive a knowledge of the owner as it was possible to gain from footprints. He had the size and shape of the boot worn, he had the length of the walking stride, and he had the length of the running stride.

Not much in itself, it is true, but in the hands of a man like Blake a good deal. From it he could—and would—read much. He chose to re-enter the house by way of the basement window, but before doing so he turned to the butler and spoke, "I think you said, Barker, that you admitted the man who called on your late master last night?"

"Yes, sir."

"How big a man would you say he was?"

"Well, sir, I should judge he was about the size of the master."

"Ah! I should say the late Mr. Jefferson was a man about five feet ten in height —or thereabouts."

"Just about that, sir."

"H'm! All right, Parker, we will go in now."

As he spoke Blake crawled back through the window and dropped to the floor beneath. When the butler stood beside him he turned and made his way back to the library above. Mott still sat at the desk poring over the papers, but he pushed them aside and looked up as Blake entered.

"Well, Mr. Blake, what luck? Did you find anything of interest at the back?"

"I found the footprints of the man who was here when the sergeant and his men entered," replied Blake evasively.

"I don't suppose that tells you much, does it?"

"They are not exactly an encyclopaedia of information on the subject," smiled Blake. "Still, one never knows. But I just came in for a moment before leaving. I have seen all there is to be seen here at present. I wish to see Inspector Thomas, and get from him a few facts which he possesses. Are you leaving soon?"

"In about ten minutes."

"Very well. If anything of an important nature comes up I shall let you know."

"All right; thanks. I wish you luck in your quest."

Blake advanced to shake hands, and, as he did so, came close to the desk. Unconsciously his eyes swept the conglomeration of material which the lawyer had taken from the drawers and laid there, and on one thing his gaze became concentrated for the barest fraction of a second.

It had passed on again, however, and when he looked info Mott's eyes the latter was totally unaware that anything on the desk had caused Blake any interest.

Nor did Blake make the mistake of referring to it then. Instead, he spoke of several other matters first, and only when he turned as though to go did he allow his arm to sweep carelessly over the desk. Mott did not see its course, but even if he had he would not have seen Blake's fingers abstract a small object from the midst of the several there, so neatly did he do it, and so cleverly did he palm it. Then he made for the door and passed out.

Blake's first move after leaving the house was to make for Scotland Yard. As he anticipated, he found Inspector Thomas in his office, struggling with the material he had gathered relating to the latest mystery which had been added to his already-harassed mind.

"Well, how goes it?" asked Blake, as he entered, though a glance at the inspector's lugubrious countenance was sufficient to answer for him.

"It doesn't go at all," replied the inspector.

"Have you found any traces yet of the two men who were at 12A, Fulton Terrace, last night?"

"Not yet. But we don't know so far whether there were two separate individuals there, or whether the man surprised by Sergeant Mullin was the same man who was there earlier in the evening,"

"I can set your mind at rest on that score," said Blake quietly. "They were two separate and distinct individuals."

"How do you know that?" asked the inspector, with surprise.

"I know it for a fact," replied Blake non-committally. "But before we go any further, I had better tell you that we are liable to run up against each other in this case."

"How is that?"

"Because Miss Jefferson, the niece of the murdered man, has retained me in the matter."

"The deuce she has!" grunted the inspector. "That means you have come here for information?" he added shrewdly.

"Right first time!" laughed Blake.

"What is it you want to know?"

"I want to know if you have taken steps yet to trace the boy who brought the mysterious note to the Yard last night."

"Ah, you thought we shouldn't do that!" exclaimed the inspector. "Well, we have."

"Did you get from him a description of the man who handed him the note?"

Inspector Thomas nodded.

"Yes."

"Do you mind telling me what it was?"

"It was pretty hazy, but enough to tell us one thing."

"What was that it?"

"That the man who left Jefferson's house last night about ten-thirty, and the man who handed the boy the note, were one and the same person, as you suggested was possible."

"Ah! There is no doubt on that score?"

"Well, the boy says the man who gave him the note was fairly tall, that he had no overcoat, and that he wore a soft hat pulled down over his eyes. He thought the hat was black. That coincides sufficiently with the butler's description of the man who called on Jefferson for us to figure, when we also consider the question of time, that it was the same man."

"It seems most likely," remarked Blake thoughtfully.

"I have been thinking over something you said in the library at Fulton Terrace last night," pursued the inspector.

"What is that?"

"It is this. If the man who left the house about ten-thirty, and the man who handed the note to the boy in Knightsbridge, were one and the same individual, then it doesn't seem possible that he could have been the murderer.

"Your point was, that had he been the murderer it is hardly likely he would be the means of bringing the police to the house. On the contrary, as you suggested, it would be to his interest to keep the thing quiet as long as possible."

"I remember making that point," responded Blake. "I must say that, so far, it seems a good one, too, but don't let us build too much on that, inspector. Frankly, in the present case I think each should do all he can to assist the other.

"In my opinion we are up against something of a more than ordinarily deep nature, and, unless I am greatly mistaken, it is going to take all our wits to ferret out the truth, and track down the murderer. There is one point which occurs to me, but I suppose it will be necessary to get hold of the boy who brought the note in order to throw any light on it."

"What is it?"

"If you will remember, his story is that the man who gave him the note also gave him a sovereign."

"Yes."

"What I wish to find out is, if the boy knows whether the man seemed plentifully supplied with money or not."

"As it happens I can answer that. When the boy was telling his story he said the man pulled out a handful of gold, and from the lot took the sovereign which he gave the boy."

"Ah, that is fortunate! We know then that though the man who looked like a wharf labourer visited Jefferson's house without wearing an overcoat on a very wet night, when he left the house he was plentifully supplied with gold coins."

"Which seems to endorse my theory that robbery was the motive," interrupted the inspector.

"Yet not five minutes ago you said you did not think that man was the murderer," laughed Blake.

"Oh, hang it all, I don't know what I think!" grunted the inspector, flushing. "Sometimes I think he is, and sometimes I think he isn't. I get into such a maze I don't know where I am."

"Of one thing, you can be sure," said Blake. "That man of mystery knows as much about this murder as any living being. Whether he did the deed or not is a different matter.

"But I said last night, and I say now —find that man. I don't mind saying, inspector, that I have run across two or three bits of information which are at your disposal if you wish."

"Ah, I shall be glad to have them!"

"Very well. Firstly, I have discovered that two days before his death Gilbert Jefferson drew from the bank twenty thousand pounds in gold.

"Secondly, I have discovered that not the slightest trace of that gold, or the purpose for which it may have been used, can be discovered amongst the papers referring to the dead man's estate.

"Thirdly, I have discovered the fact that the man who visited Jefferson during the evening was not the man who was surprised in the study by Sergeant Mullin. As yet, I have not made any deductions from those facts, but, such as they are, you are welcome to them."

"Good heavens!" cried the inspector, half rising from his chair, "Are you sure of that about the twenty thousand pounds?"

"Do I usually make statements unless I am sure of them?" asked Blake drily.

"No, no, I didn't mean that. But don't you see what it does?"

"What?"

"Why, it proves beyond the shadow of a doubt that my first theory that robbery was the motive is the correct one after all."

"And which man do you suspect as being the murderer?"

"That I don't know," replied the inspector grimly, "but you can wager on this. If the two men who were at Fulton Terrace last night are in England, my men will have them gathered in within a week, and once we get them I guess we will find out which one did the job."

"I am sure I hope so," answered Blake, as he rose. "By the way, do you remember when you were at my rooms last evening we were discussing the murders which had taken place recently, and which seemed to baffle solution?"

"Yes."

"Then you will remember that we discussed the murder of Mr. Herbert Welkin, M.P., which took place as he was walking home from his club?"

"Certainly."

"And you will recollect that in telling me of it you mentioned the objects found in his pockets during the examination."

"Yes."

"Am I right in thinking that you said you found a small ebony skull about the size of a filbert, and fashioned after a human skull?"

"Yes. We discovered afterwards that Mr. Welkin was an amateur collector, and judged it to be an object from his collection which he may have carried as a mascot. Lots of collectors have fads of that nature. Why do you ask?"

"Because I wished to know if you have it now."

"Yes. It is with a few other articles of his which we still have here at the Yard."

"Do you mind letting me have it for a day or two? I wish to make an examination of it, and also endeavour to trace its history if I can. I am, as you know, something of a collector myself; but I must confess I am ignorant as to the period and origin or that small ebony skull."

"Then you are going on with the investigation of the murders we discussed as well as this one?" asked the inspector.

"I certainly am," answered Blake.

"Then I shall let you have it. I am glad you are not shelving those other murders. As I told you last night, I shall greatly appreciate any assistance you give me. If I fail to trace the perpetrator of this latest crime as well—whew! it will be mine for the simple life all right, all right. I will get the skull for you in a moment."

The inspector rose and left the room, evidently to get the little skull which Blake wished to have. As the door closed after him, Blake leaned back and murmured:

"It can do no possible good at present to tell him I found one of those ebony skulls at Fulton Terrace. Until I know what they mean, and whether between the murder at Fulton or whether they form any connection Terrace and the murder of Herbert Welkin, M.P. the possession of one by each of the men in the two cases is purely a coincidence, it is useless to seriously consider them. Still, it was odd to see one on Jefferson's desk, and I hope Mott doesn't miss it."

At that moment the inspector returned and held out a tiny black skull to Blake. It was no larger than a good-sized filbert, was fashioned after the style of the human skull, and, as he took it, Blake noticed with a quick thrill, that its teeth were of ivory.

In size, colour, and form, it was an exact duplicate of the one he had so cleverly palmed in the study of 12A, Fulton Terrace, less than an hour before. He slipped it carelessly into his pocket, and, after making arrangements to communicate with the inspector at once did anything particular develop, he made his way out.

Hailing a taxi, Blake told the driver to go to Baker Street, and sinking back in the corner, he closed his eyes in thought. He did not open them again until the stopping of the taxi told him he had reached his destination.

Then he jumped out and, paying the man, hurried up the steps. He found Tinker at work over the Index, with Pedro stretched out at the lad's feet.

Tinker looked up as Blake entered and opened his mouth to speak, but Blake cut him short,

"Stir yourself, my lad!" he rapped. "Get into the disguise of a street lad as quickly as possible. I have some shadowing for you to do, and there is no time to be lost."

Tinker rose to obey, and hurried from the consulting-room. No sooner was he gone than Blake seated himself and drew out his notebook. Laying it before him, he drew towards him a pad of paper, and picking up his pencil began to elaborate on the notes and measurements he had taken.

He was interrupted very shortly by the entry of Tinker, who had lost no time in garbing himself as Blake had ordered. The detective lifted his head and spoke curtly.

"You will go at once to Fulton Terrace, and keep a watch on 12A. Take note of everyone who enters and leaves. You may run up against a plain-clothes man, because Inspector Thomas is also on the case. If so, it will be as well to make yourself known to him.

"You had better send word to Tim, the lad in Soho whom you sometimes get to assist you. He can keep a lookout at the back, and if it is necessary for you to follow anyone, or to return here to report, he can relieve you. Understand, this is a tough case, and as a matter of professional pride, we want to beat the police.

"I depend on you to keep your eyes and ears open, and not to miss a thing of value. If you see anyone or anything of a suspicions nature, follow it up, and report here at once. That is all. Now go along."

Almost ere Blake had finished speaking the door had closed behind Tinker, and a moment later the street-door slammed as he raced out on his mission. When he was gone, Blake returned to his work, and for half an hour only the steady sound of pencil on paper broke the silence of the consulting-room.

At the end of that time he lifted his head and drew towards him the sheets of paper which he had covered with writing. What he had written was an elaboration of the notes and information he had gathered, together with a certain amount of analysis and deduction, and in substance it was as follows:

"Case:

"Murder of a man at 12A, Fulton Terrace."

Then followed a detailed account of the finding of the body the previous night, and the evidence at the inquest the next day. From that it continued:

"Gilbert Jefferson had two visitors the night of the murder —one a bidden guest, the other an unbidden guest. The former arrives without coat or umbrella, though the night is stormy. From butler's description he might he a dock labourer.

"Evidence seems to show that he left about ten-thirty. Further evidence shows that he was the man who was in Knightsbridge a quarter of an hour later, and who gave a boy a mysterious note to take to Scotland Yard.

"Evidence does not show what money he possessed when he arrived at Fulton Terrace, but it does prove that he was plentifully supplied with gold when in Knightsbridge at a quarter to eleven.

"Query:

"What is the explanation of this?

"If he was in possession of the gold before his arrival at Fulton Terrace, why was his garb apparently of such a nature as to cause the butler to look upon him as a labouring man, and to lead one to think the absence of overcoat or umbrella was due to his financial inability to purchase those articles?

"Next comes the mysterious note itself. The wording is striking when analysed. It shows undoubted signs of having been written under stress, and exhibits a subconscious reflex of the sense of location.

"One word alone proves it was written within the house in Fulton Terrace. That word is the word 'come.' Had it been written outside, it would have said 'go.' Proof seems to show that it was written by Gilbert Jefferson.

"Query:

"Was the note written by him and given to his visitor to send to the Yard after leaving the house? If so, did he anticipate any danger approaching him that night? If the latter is the case, why did he send for the police in the way he did?

"Why didn't he telephone, and keep his visitor there to assist him in case anything occurred? If he anticipated danger, had the presence of the second individual there at midnight anything to do with it?

"The bulk of the evidence seems to point to the man who sent the note having left the house before the murder, yet other facts make the opposite appear the case.

"Query:

"Who was the individual surprised in the study about midnight by the police?

"It seems certain that he was ignorant of the fact that a note had been sent to Scotland Yard summoning the police. Had the contrary been the case, he would never have risked an entry.

"Was he the murderer? Did he enter by premeditation, or was his presence there merely a coincidence? If a coincidence, he never committed the murder, for that deed was premeditated.

"The note, for one thing, shows something sinister was in the air, and the fact that the face and hands of the murdered man were disfigured by acid proves the premeditation. And that brings another query.

"Why was this mutilation committed? The absence of any great disorder in the room proves that the dead man made no violent struggle, and also proves that the murderer was not in an uncontrollable rage, which might lead him to mutilate the body after he had committed the deed. This points to premeditation as well as the murder itself.

"Query:

"Why should a murderer wish to disfigure beyond recognition the features of the person he had killed?

"The question itself supplies the answer —to prevent recognition.

"And in all the evidence of identification, the dead man was identified as Gilbert Jefferson by his clothes, the contents of his pockets, and the mark where a ring had been on one finger.

"Again, to return to the individual who was surprised by the police. My mould of the footprint shows that this individual possessed a remarkably small foot for a man.

"The size of the foot and the deduction that the owner must be of small stature is endorsed by my measurements of the stride. These are even more striking than the size of the footprint.

"From computation I find that the owner must have been no more than five feet six in height. Yet here comes a discrepancy.

The average man of that height has a much longer stride than those I have examined.

"Therefore, even though it appears against the proof of mathematical deduction, it seems that the owner must have been of an even smaller stature. The stride, when considered alone, points to a man's height of barely five feet two, yet, on the other hand, a man of only that height would hardly have feet as large as those which caused the imprints.

"Referring to past cases, and considering the evidence furnished by them, another alternative presents itself. It is this:

"Is it possible that the owner of the feet which made the imprints which I have examined was not a dwarf with large feet, or a short-statured man with remarkably small feet, a woman who was wearing heavy boots made large, and fashioned as those of a man. This would explain not only the size but the length of stride.

"Another thing which seems to point to this supposition is the length of the running stride which goes from the library window to the wall.

"From the study I have made of the actions of the human body, both when the mind is tranquil and when it is excited, I must say the running stride which I examined would be far more difficult to reconcile with a male owner.

"But even more than the walking stride do they fit the theory that they were owned by a woman. This is further endorsed by their short, nervous nature.

"Query:

"Was the owner a deformed male or a woman? If the latter, what was she doing in Gilbert Jefferson's library at midnight? It seems unlikely that a woman would dress in the garments of a man and go there without premeditation. But does that premeditation argue that she —presuming it was a she —had anything to do with the murder?

"The next point to be explained is, what has become of the twenty thousand pounds in gold which Gilbert Jefferson drew from the bank?

"Query:

"Why did he draw it in gold?

"Furthermore, the financier, Hammerton Palmer, may be able to throw some light on the matter.

"Query:

"Why was he not present at the inquest?

"Note:

"Make a thorough analysis of Gilbert Jefferson's will.

"Note:

"Make a thorough research regarding the two black ebony skulls.

"Query:

"What, if any, is their meaning, and does the possession of one each by two men of mystery contain any important suggestion."

This is exactly how far Blake had got when he stopped writing, and began to read over what he had written. He had barely finished, and was still frowning over the mass of points and questions raised, when the desk 'phone rang loudly.

Reaching over, he drew it towards him, and lifted the receiver. No sooner had he done so, and said "Hallo!" than the voice at the other end answered him, and he recognised it as that of Alice Jefferson, saying:

"Is that Mr. Blake speaking?"

"Yes," answered Blake.

"Then I must tell you that I am afraid I have broken my promise. I have just had a caller, and I let slip the fact that you were on the case."

"ONE moment," said Blake. "Do I understand you to say that you have had a visitor, and to that visitor you acknowledged that I was on the case?"

"Yes; but really, Mr. Blake, it came out before I thought. In fact, it happened before I knew it, and —"

"Wait, please. Tell me first, who was your caller?"

"Hammerton Palmer, the financier."

"Ah! When did he call?"

"Very shortly after you left."

"Then he has not gone long?"

"No. I rang you up almost as soon as he departed. I should say he has been gone less than a quarter of an hour."

"I think you had better tell me, as briefly as possible, just what passed while he was there," said Blake, after a short pause. "Don't say too much over the 'phone. If you speak in general terms I shall understand."

"Well, Mr. Blake, I had just said good-bye to Mr. Mott when Mr. Palmer called. I came down at once. He said he had just reached the City, and had come direct to the house. After he had condoled with me, he asked if he could be of any assistance to me. I thanked him, and told him, Mr. Mott was looking after things for me.

"I then asked him if he knew he was to benefit by uncle's will and be said he had known for some time. He added that he had assisted uncle financially, and that the inclusion of him in the will had been merely a safeguard in case uncle died before the money was repaid.

"He then asked what was being done to bring the perpetrators of the crime to justice. I told him the police were on the matter, and he said he thought we should get a good private detective. Then he mentioned your name, saying it might be a good idea to consult you.

"That was when I let it slip that I had already seen you, and that you had taken the case. After that we talked of uncle's affairs, though I didn't know many details. I mentioned that the estate was twenty thousand pounds short, and —"

"What!" almost shouted Blake. "Say that again, please."

"I told him the estate was twenty thousand pounds short. Surely there was no harm in that, was there?"

"What did he say?" asked Blake, in a voice of deadly calm.

"He seemed very much astonished. In fact, he said it must be impossible, and that we must find it eventually."

"Did he question you very closely on the matter?"

"Now that I think of it, he did, though I don't see why he should have worried. It is to be repaid out of my share of the estate."

"Exactly. Well, Miss Jefferson, I am sorry in a way that this has occurred, but perhaps no harm has been done. If you are asked any questions after this, I think the best plan would be for you to refer all inquiries to Mr. Mott. He will know how to deal with them as they should be dealt with. I think you should refuse yourself to all callers for a few days, at least."

"I promise you I shall, Mr. Blake. I hope you don't think I have done very wrong."

"Oh, don't worry over it, Miss Jefferson. What is done can't be helped. Only, please be more careful in future. And now I shall ring off. I hear the bell, and imagine I have a caller myself. Good-bye. You may hear from me again very soon."

As he finished speaking, Blake hung up the receiver. Barely had he done so when the door of the consulting-room opened, and Mrs. Bardell ushered in a visitor.

He was a man of medium height, well set up, and well groomed. His face was half-hidden by a moustache and pointed beard, plentifully besprinkled with grey. Gold pince-nez were perched on his nose, giving him a distinctly scholarly look, but at the first glance Blake knew him by the many pictures he had seen of him. It was no scholar, but the powerful and well-known City financier, Hammerton Palmer.

As Blake bowed, he reflected that the financier must have come to Baker Street direct from Fulton Terrace —a reflection which was perfectly correct. As a matter of fact, he had been on his way even as Blake had been listening over the 'phone to the details of his call on Alice Jefferson.

He advanced into the room, and gazed straight into Blake's eyes.

"I needn't ask if this is Mr. Sexton Blake," he said, with a smile. "I should recognise you at once by your pictures."

Again Blake bowed.

"You have made no mistake in your inference, Mr. —"

"Palmer," said the other, with a faint laugh. "I see my pictures have hardly done as much for me as yours have for you; but perhaps my name has reached you —Hammerton Palmer?"

"Ah! Mr. Palmer," replied Blake, without the faintest hint that he had known his visitor's identity from the first. "Won't you sit down? What is it I can do for you?"

"To tell you the truth, Mr. Blake, I have not come to ask you to take a case, but to offer you my poor services in a case which, I am told, you have just undertaken."

"Indeed! What case is that, Mr. Palmer?"

"I speak of the terrible murder of my friend Gilbert Jefferson."

"Who told you I was on the case?"

"Miss Jefferson. I've only just arrived in the City, otherwise I should have gone to see her before. In fact, I came on as soon as I heard of the awful affair. Naturally, I went round at once to offer her my services, and as soon as I heard you had matters in hand, I came to see you.

"Needless to say, I am anxious to do all in my power to run down the scoundrels who have done this thing, and any resources, financial or otherwise, which I have, are at your disposal, Mr. Blake. It struck me that, with your brains and my influence, we ought to be able to put our hands on the perpetrators within a reasonable space of time."

"Your offer is very kind, I am sure," said Blake evenly. "As you know, however, I am engaged by Miss Jefferson, and if I fail to catch the person or persons who have committed the crime, her finances will not be strained. By the way, Mr. Palmer, you spoke of scoundrels in the plural. Is it, then, your idea that more than one individual was engaged in this affair!"

For a fleeting second Blake could have sworn that a look almost of savage rage appeared in the eyes of the other, but so quickly did it pass, that, a moment later, he could not be sure he had really seen it. At any rate, when the financier spoke again, his tones were as cool and even as those of Blake.

"Of course, I have not given much thought to the matter, Mr. Blake. When I spoke of scoundrels, I did not particularly mean one or more persons. What do you think yourself?"

Blake shrugged.

"I haven't got that far yet, Mr. Palmer."

"By the way," went on the financier, "I suppose you know the terms of the will?"

"Oh, yes I understand you are to benefit to the extent of forty thousand pounds."

"Yes. That was a precaution taken in case Jefferson should die before he cleared off his indebtedness to me. You know I loaned him that amount some months ago, when he was hard pushed for money."

"So Mr. Mott seemed to think," answered Blake.

"Rather a strange thing that twenty thousand pounds in gold should be missing from the estate, don't you think?" said the financier carelessly, looking down at his nails.

Blake rose and strolled across to the window, where he stood looking out for a few moments; then he turned, and, leaning against the sill, looked at the other.

"I don't know that I should call it strange," he answered slowly. "For instance, there may be several explanations of it. I suppose you know the details of it?"

"Yes."

"What is your own idea?"

"I —I don't know, Mr. Blake. I can't explain it. It was a queer thing to do in the first place. Then consider that he drew it all in gold. Gold can't be traced, whereas notes can."

"Exactly. But don't you think it possible Mr. Jefferson may have had some private debt which he wished to pay off before his death?"

"He may have had," admitted the financier.

And as he spoke those few words, he never noticed the sudden steely glitter which flashed in Blake's eyes.

"Then my offer of assistance is not accepted, Mr. Blake?"

"I am afraid there is nothing you can do just at present, Mr. Palmer. If there should be, I shall call on you with pleasure. But rest assured, no efforts will be spared to hunt down the person or persons who have committed this crime. Be their position high or low, they will pay the penalty if they are tracked down."

"Then you think you will succeed? Have you any clues?"

"It is too early in the game yet to talk of success or failure, Mr. Palmer. As to clues, there are always clues —some sound, some unsound. But my experience has been that no crime was ever committed without a clue of some sort existing. The puzzle is to follow such clue or clues until the right person is reached."

"Well, I am sure I wish you every success, Sir. Blake," said the financier, as he rose. "Don't forget, I am always at your service. The least I can do is to assist in some way to track down the murderers of my old friend."

As he spoke he walked past the desk to where Blake stood and held out his hand. Blake took it, and after a few more words, ushered out his visitor.

When he was gone, Blake returned to the window, and stood gazing out thoughtfully for some time. He saw Hammerton Palmer enter a luxurious car which was waiting at the kerb, and drive off. Then Blake walked to the desk and sank into his chair,

"Like a good many people, you leave the real object of your visit until the last, Mr. Palmer," he muttered slowly. "All your conversation was but a preamble leading up to the point. That point you finally reached, and unless I am greatly mistaken, it was to learn what you could regarding the missing twenty thousand pounds.

"When I first considered the matter, and reflected how you seemed to be mixed up financially with Gilbert Jefferson, I dealt with the possibility of your having been the recipient of the gold. Now, however, I know differently. It is evident you knew nothing of that until Miss Jefferson told you.

"Then why were you so anxious to find out what I knew or thought about it? That was the main reason for your coming hot foot from Fulton Terrace to Baker Street. But far greater than that is something which happened during your visit, Mr. Palmer, and I'll wager you don't know yet what it was.

"When I was speaking of the gold, I deliberately asked you if it was not possible that Mr. Jefferson may have had some private debt to pay off before his death, intimating that he must have been anticipating death.

"Your answer was that he might have had such a debt, admitting unconsciously that Gilbert Jefferson did anticipate death and that you knew it.

"What is the meaning of that? What death did Gilbert Jefferson expect? Why and how does it happen that Hammerton Palmer also knew it? No amount of denial can ever sweep away that one unconscious admission made in those few simple words.

"I have felt certain all along that there was something of a deep and complicated nature behind all this, and now I am absolutely certain of it. I would give a good deal to know as much about this affair as you know, Mr. Palmer. But we shall see what we shall see."

As he mused, Blake's eyes had been roving aimlessly about the desk, but as his thoughts reached this point they broke off suddenly, and a frown of irritation appeared on his face as his gaze became fixed on a small ashtray directly in front of him.

Slowly his hand went out until his fingers grasped something which lay in the tray, and slowly he lifted the object up, the frown still clouding his features.

"If I hadn't seen this with my own eyes, I should have said it was impossible for me to be so careless," he muttered. "Whatever possessed me to leave this of all things in plain sight on the desk?"

It was a tiny black ebony skull which he had picked up, and which, to judge from his remarks, he had evidently laid in the tray instead of returning it to his pocket.

"Now, I could have sworn that I placed both of them in my pocket," he went on. "It is odd how I could have put one back, and left the other on the desk. At any rate, I shall see that it does not occur again."

At this point, he thrust his fingers in his waistcoat pocket, and brought them out slowly, to reveal not the one skull he had expected to find, but two. Like a flash, he was on his feet, his eyes narrowing, his nostrils quivering like those of a racehorse.

In his hand were three tiny black skulls. He had made no mistake. He had returned both the skulls he had possessed to his pocket. The third one had appeared from somewhere else.

And even as the thought occurred, he muttered grimly:

"That skull was left here by Hammerton Palmer when he crossed to take his leave of me. What does it mean? Has he thrown down the gage of battle? Am I, too, sentenced to death? What is it? What is behind all this?

"Is Hammerton Palmer, after all, the secret at one end of the puzzle? If he is, he feels deadly certain of himself and his ability to protect himself.

"If he is the solution, I swear not all his influence or his money will save him. But this skull means danger —danger quick and sure unless I move warily.

"So be it. The fight is on. We shall see who wins."

**Yvonne was curled up in a chair in the smoking-room reading all the latest editions of the papers, and pondering over the mystery.** (*Chapter 6.*)

LITTLE did Yvonne know how sinister and mysterious she loomed in the calculations of the police. It will be remembered that when she escaped over the rear wall back of the Jeffersons' place she reached her car in safety, and, owing to Alec's prompt actions, made good her escape.

It will also be recalled that no sooner did she recover her breath, than a thousand and one doubts began to torture her mind.

She sat in silence all the way home, and when, after effectually shaking off all signs of pursuit, Alec drew up in front of the house at Queen Anne's Gate, she bade him a brief good-night, and hastened in. A light still burned in the room at the end of the hall, and the sound of pacing footsteps told her Graves was still up waiting for her.

Nor did the anxiety he betrayed by that restless pacing ease Yvonne's mind. For the moment she found it utterly impossible to meet him. She felt an imperative desire for the solitude of her room, where she could think things out calmly.

As he heard her in the hall, Graves stopped his pacing, and she could see his shadow against the light as he approached the door of the smoking-room. Yvonne called out that she would be down presently, and, turning, sped up the stairs.

Once in her room, she closed and locked the door. Then, stirring up the fire in the grate, she doffed the sodden garments she was wearing and slipped into some soft, dry feminine attire.

Slipping her feet into a tiny pair of morocco slippers, she sank down in a chair before the fire, and let her chin sink into her hands. Then she gave her mind to the developments of the evening.

Slowly, but thoroughly, she pieced together each item until she had a fairly decipherable whole. She harked back to her interview with Channing, the interview which had inspired her determination to make a secret visit to the house of Gilbert Jefferson.

She moved on to the point where her uncle had entered, and how, after Channing's departure, she had stated to Grave's her intention. She remembered vividly how he had seemed wholly amenable to her plan until he heard whose house it was she intended to visit.

And now she shivered as she reflected how startlingly sudden had been his change of manner when he did know. She remembered his ashen pallor and his quivering tones —the almost frantic appeal he had made for her not to go, and his reiteration of the plea that she should wait at least until the morrow.

Then, once again, as she had done on her homeward way, she thought of his words to her, in which he warned her not to proceed if there were any signs of commotion about the place, Further, she reflected that he had stated positively he had not been personally acquainted with Gilbert Jefferson.

Unconsciously she began to check off her uncle's movements that evening. He had dined, so he said, at the club. He had come in about eleven, and she had to confess that until the question of her midnight visit arose he appeared perfectly normal. She asked herself who the dead man could be. Was it Gilbert Jefferson? She would know surely on the morrow.

But, insistent in her brain drummed the torturing questions. How did Graves know she might find something terrible in that house of mystery? How did he know there might be a commotion? By commotion, had he meant invasion of police? For, know he did, Yvonne felt certain.

Then why —why —why? That the man she had discovered had been murdered there could be no doubt. Then what had Graves, her uncle, to do with a man found murdered in the study of Gilbert Jefferson's house?

Though her breast was torn with miserable imaginings, Yvonne could not bring herself to think that Graves had struck down a fellow man. She knew his indolent, easy-going nature too well.

Since her mother's death he had been all she had left, and from the time of her daring course of vengeance against the men who had ruined herself and her mother in Australia, they had not only been in the position of uncle and niece, but in that of comrades as well.

Still, though he may not have had any hand in the deed himself, he knew something about it, and that something might lead to complications of a serious nature. Even she herself might find it extremely difficult to explain her presence in Gilbert Jefferson's house at midnight, were that fact discovered and her identity traced.

At this point in her thoughts a low knock came at the door, and a moment later she heard Graves' voice.

"Are you coming down, Yvonne?" he called.

With a weary shrug of the shoulders, she rose.

"Yes, in five minutes," she answered.

"All right; I shall wait in the smoking-room," was his reply.

She leaned against the dressing-table as she heard his departing footsteps, then, giving herself a shake, she straightened up, and moved slowly towards the door. There was nothing for it but to face the thing now.

And, indicative is it of Yvonne's nature, that as she turned the key, she murmured:

"If he does know anything about this affair, he must tell me who has a hand in it. Shrewder brains than his may throw the arrow of suspicion to point to him. In that case, he must be protected."

She walked swiftly to the head of the stairs and descended. In the smoking-room Graves was standing beside the desk, lighting a cigar. Yvonne noticed in one swift glance that his face was still pale, and that the hand which held the match was far from steady.

Then she herself selected a small cigarette from the box on the desk, and, sinking into a chair lighted it. She maintained a resolute silence, determined that he should speak first. And speak he did, in tones tinged with hoarseness.

"How did you make out?" he asked, without turning round.

"Is that a necessary question, uncle?" she asked quietly.

The match dropped from Graves' hand, and he swung round sharply.

"My heavens, Yvonne!" he gasped, "tell me, what did you find?"

Yvonne gazed into his eyes mercilessly, then she spoke in slow, even tones.

"You ask me what I found? I will tell you. I found first a house of darkness. I found the study as I had planned. Then I found something of a very different nature. I found a man in that study sitting before the desk. But that man was a corpse. He had been struck down even as he sat there."

Then suddenly Yvonne leaned forward, and her blue eyes seemed to burn into Graves' soul, as, with a sudden change of tone, she said sharply:

"Was that man Gilbert Jefferson?"

"My heavens! —yes!" gasped Graves, tottering to a chair.

In a moment Yvonne was on her feet.

"You must tell me what you mean by that, uncle," she said, in tones strangely hard. "You knew of that murder before I went there. Rather than tell me then what you knew, you permitted me to go. I escaped by a bare ten seconds from falling into the hands of the police.

"Think what my position would have been had I not done so. Think what construction would have been placed upon my being found there, garbed in masculine garments, with a murdered man in the room!

"And yet, by your own words, before I went you showed you knew what I was liable to find. You knew the risks I ran. Still, you refused to speak your reasons for begging me not to go. And just now you have confessed that the man who was murdered was Gilbert Jefferson. Don't you see the urgency of the whole affair? Don't you see your own peril? Don't you see my peril?"

Graves groaned, and looked up with haggard eyes.

"Listen, Yvonne," he said. "I swear to you I had no hand in that affair. You know it would be impossible for me to strike down a man in cold blood. But —but I did know death threatened Gilbert Jefferson, and I knew he would meet his death to-night. It was not murder I anticipated, but suicide.

"That, however, is all I can tell you. Could I have said more I should have done so before you went. Had you been anyone else I would have held you back by force, if necessary; but I trusted to your own cleverness to keep you free of danger. All the time you were gone I was nearly mad with worry. Half a dozen times I started after you, then drew back, afraid I might miss you.

"And now ask me no more, I beseech you, for I have already said far more than I should. Believe me, Yvonne, I am bound as by bands of iron, and even if I would say more, I cannot —I dare not. As to peril, there is none for you or for me. The cause of Gilbert Jefferson's death will never be discovered."

Yvonne had listened in silence to her uncle's vehement outburst. When he had finished, she tossed her cigarette into the grate and rose.

"Very well, uncle," she said quietly. "You must, of course, follow your own inclination as to whether you tell me what you know or not. To me, you seem like a man overridden by fear. You say there is no peril for you or for me. That remains to be seen. Personally, I think otherwise.

"But if there is anything threatening you, you would be wise to confide in me. You know my resources, both financial and otherwise. If this affair and your fear are part and parcel of some old indiscretion, make a clean breast of it. I will give you all the assistance in my power. Together we can meet that which you fear so much, and vanquish it. Won't you trust me?"

"I cannot, Yvonne. I am bound."

"Very well. Let me say this, however. I intend following up this affair, and if success attend my efforts I will find out the truth anyway."

With that, she turned and passed from the room, leaving Graves sitting in his chair, with head bowed in his hands.


Yvonne was awake early the next morning, and sent Anna her maid out for the papers at once. She read the brief references to the crime and, on discovering the hour of the inquest, dressed at once. She was there during all the evidence, and none who saw the heavily-veiled woman sitting in a shadowy corner of the room dreamed of connecting her with the affair.

She heard all the evidence of the servants and the police. She heard Blake endorse the remarks of Inspector Thomas and, just before the inquest was concluded; she slipped out quietly in order not to meet Blake face to face.

She returned at once to Queen Anne's Gate, and even while Blake was at Fulton Terrace making his first detailed examination of the library and grounds, she was curled up in a chair in the smoking-room reading all the latest editions of the papers, and pondering over the mystery.

One enterprising reporter had ferreted out the terms of the will, and at the very moment when Hammerton Palmer was interviewing Blake at Baker Street, an edition appeared on the streets proclaiming the financier's share in the estate of Gilbert Jefferson.

When she had procured this edition and read the medley of facts and fancies which it contained, Yvonne rose and put on her things.

"Since I am the second largest shareholder in the Jefferson Silk Company, I think it would be as well for me to make a personal visit to the offices and find out exactly how we stand over the affair," she murmured.

She had just 'phoned for the car when there came a ring at the bell, and a moment later Channing was announced.

"I thought perhaps you might wish to go down to the offices, Mademoiselle Yvonne," he said after greeting her. "I came round to accompany you in case you did."

"I am very glad," answered Yvonne. "I was just starting for there, and have been wishing I knew where to get hold of you."

They passed out together and entered the car, discussing the startling events which had occurred since Channing had departed from Queen Anne's Gate the previous evening.

At the offices of the Jefferson Silk Company they found everything in confusion. The place was closed for business, and the blinds were drawn, but, after a sharp summons, Yvonne and Channing were admitted.

They found Formby Mott, the lawyer, and one of the executors of the will, in the office formerly used by Gilbert Jefferson. With him was the secretary of the company, an elderly man named Johnson, who had been named by Jefferson as the other executor.

They rose at once as Yvonne entered, and Johnson, who knew her, introduced her to Mott. After shaking hands, she seated herself and turned to the lawyer.

"I presume you know I am one of the shareholders in the Jefferson Silk Company, Mr. Mott?"

The lawyer bowed.

"Am I to understand that the terms of the will will be complied with? Are the affairs of the late Mr. Jefferson in good order?"

"They are not in perfect order," answered Mott, "but, in general, it will be possible to carry out the terms. The company will not suffer at all —the deficiency being provided for out of the share due to his niece."

"Then there is a deficiency?"

"Yes."

Then Mott told her of the missing twenty thousand pounds, and Yvonne listened as closely as though she had not already had the full details from Channing. When the lawyer had finished, she said:

"I understand that this dividing of Mr. Jefferson's shares between Miss Jefferson and Hammerton Palmer, the financier, will leave me as the biggest individual shareholder in the company?"

"That is quite true."

"Then I think, Mr. Johnson, you had better call a meeting of the shareholders as soon as possible."

The secretary flushed.

"Er —er —the fact is, Mr. Palmer was here less than ten minutes before you arrived, and gave me instructions not to call a meeting until he directed, mademoiselle."

"But I am a larger shareholder than he is. In fact, I am now the controlling interest in the firm."

"Well, technically, yes; but Mr. Palmer stated that Miss Jefferson would vote her shares with his, thus giving him control of the business."

"Ah! I see that Mr. Palmer is losing no time. But I refuse to recognise his right to give any such orders, Mr. Johnson. I still stand on my position, and demand that a meeting be called."

"When Mr. Palmer made the statement that Miss Jefferson would vote her shares with his, I asked him on what authority he made the statement," put in Mott. "He replied that he had a document duly made out by the late Gilbert Jefferson, and witnessed before a lawyer, charging his niece, in case of his death, to be guided in her dealings with the Silk Company by Hammerton Palmer. Mr. Palmer said he received it at the time he assisted Mr. Jefferson financially, and would produce it when required. I don't see what Miss Jefferson can do but follow her uncle's wishes."

"Since probate of the estate has not yet been taken out, it seems to me that Mr. Hammerton Palmer's assumption of authority is a little premature,'" said Yvonne coldly, as she rose. Then turning to Channing, she said: "Mr. Channing, you will please remain here to represent me. I shall count on you to advise me promptly of each development. You, Mr. Johnson, will hear further from me."

With a frigid bow to Mott she swept out; leaving the lawyer not a little puzzled, and the secretary decidedly nervous.

From the offices of the Silk Company Yvonne drove direct to Queen Anne's Gate, and it is a strange thing that, owing to entirely different reasons and by an entirely different sequence of events, her mind was full of the same man that Sexton Blake was pondering over at that very moment —Hammerton Palmer the financier.

It was well past five in the afternoon when she arrived. Graves had been out since early morning, and she had not seen him all day. A message was now waiting from him saying he would dine at the club, so, ordering an early dinner, Yvonne went to her room. At seven she dined, and at a quarter to eight she again sought her room.

Before dinner she had laid out several garments on the bed, and these she now slipped into. They comprised a dark tweed skirt and jacket, a dark blouse, and small, close-fitting hat and veil. On her feet she wore heavy walking shoes, and in the pocket of her jacket she placed a small automatic pistol.

When the hat was adjusted to her taste, and the veil wrapped round her head effectually concealing her features, she drew on her gloves, and once more sought the street. This time she did not send for the car, but started off at a brisk walk.

It was just eight-thirty when, by a series of turnings, she reached Fulton Terrace, and strolled slowly down on the opposite side from No. 12A.

As she did so she passed a man whose body was concealed by a long ulster, and whose features were almost hidden by a soft hat which was pulled well down over his eyes.

Then a moment later a street lad passed her, but so far as she could see neither of them paid any attention to her.

How utterly stupefied she would have been had she been aware of the identity of the man in the ulster, and how her pulses would have quickened had she known that the garb of the street lad hid the identity of Tinker!

But she knew neither of these things and, intent on her own purpose, kept on until she reached a dark corner where, in the shelter of a projecting wall, she took up her stand and turned her gaze in the direction of No. 12A.

**Tinker could have reached out and touched the man, so close was he.** (*Chapter 7*)

Slowly and cautiously Tinker crept forward until a dark doorway
loomed up ahead of him. He moved still closer and, crouching
down, pressed his ear hard against the door. (*Chapter 7.*)

Tinker could not retreat; he dared not advance; he could
only cling on and wait. (*Chapter 7.*)

**From the telegraph pole Tinker could see right
into the room, and see the man he had shadowed.**
(*Chapter 7.*)

A car in front of 12a was an object of interest to Tinker. He had been on the watch less than twenty minutes when a man emerged and entered it. *(Chapter 7.)*

With a startled gasp, Tinker turned to see the man he had followed standing in the doorway, gazing at him over the barrel of a steadily-held automatic pistol. (*Chapter 7.*)

WHEN Tinker left Baker Street to take up his post in Fulton Terrace, he took the precaution of sending a telegram to Tim, the Soho lad whom Tinker sometimes employed, telling him to come on to Fulton Terrace without delay.

He had barely made a careful examination of the outside of the premises, and chosen a likely spot from which to keep a watch on the house during the evening, when Tim appeared. He listened carefully to Tinker's instructions, and the latter had hardly finished speaking before Tim was away to take up his post in the rear.

A car in front of No, 12A was an object of interest to Tinker, and he kept a careful eye out for the owner who appeared to be inside. He had not long to wait to prove that this was so, for he had been on the watch less than twenty minutes when a man emerged and entered it.

As the car drove off Tinker took a mental note of the man's features, in order to describe him to Blake, but never for a moment did he guess that it was Hammerton Palmer, the financier, and that he was on his way to Baker Street.

For some time after that his watch was monotonous. Dusk settled down, and the street grew quiet. The occasional tradesman's cart which had rumbled through during the day was no more to be seen. Here and there in some of the houses lights shone, and from the basements came the sound of clattering dishes and the smell of cooking. Then that passed.

A few maids appeared in the area-way; a taxi or two came through the terrace, picked up fares for the theatre, and drove off; a policeman strolled through, stopping here and there to chatt a loitering maid; then he, too, passed from view, the maids withdrew, and the street became practically deserted.

Still Tinker remained concealed in a dark areaway. As yet he had seen no signs of the plain clothes' detective whom Blake thought Inspector Thomas might have on the scene. Still, he might be there concealed, as was Tinker. Nor had the lad heard anything from Tim, proving that so far no developments had taken place at the rear of No. 12 A.

It had just gone eight o'clock when the silence of the street was broken by a loud steady footfall at the upper end. Peering forth from his place of concealment, Tinker saw the figure of a man just turning into the street from the wider one beyond.

As he passed under a light the lad could see that he was fairly tall, and wore a long ulster with a soft cap pulled well down over his eyes. Then he broke into the shadow again, and became but a blurred, indistinct outline.

Tinker's first thought was that it might be the plain clothes' man, but his shrewd young eyes had taken rapid note of the man's bearing and gait, and he decided against that assumption. As the figure approached closer he drew back in the shadow.

He began to think now that the man must live in one of the houses in the street, but when he drew up and stood against the area railing two feet from where Tinker crouched, the lad's pulses began to hammer madly. Though he knew he ran imminent risk of discovery were he heard, Tinker held his breath and cautiously raised his head. He could have reached out and touched the man, so close was he.

He saw that the other had turned his back and was gazing intently in the direction of No. 12A. Again Tinker wondered if it might be the plain clothes' man, and he had almost made up his mind to speak when another footfall sounded up the street. The man heard it, too, and Tinker heard him mutter a curse as he turned and moved away, keeping well in the shadow.

Once more risking discovery, Tinker craned his neck and peered out. Down the opposite side of the street came the swinging figure of a man. He kept on at a brisk stride until he reached No. 12A. There he turned and, running up the steps, pressed the bell.

As he did so he raised one hand and stroked the back of his neck, and, on seeing the movement, Tinker grinned furtively, for he recognised Blake. A moment later the door opened, and he saw his master disappear within.

Hard on this incident came another footfall. The owner was coming down the other side of the street also, and barely had he taken one glance at the newcomer than Tinker grinned a second time. Walk and gait proclaimed to him the plain clothes' man, and he knew that the inspector's man had appeared at last.

But quickly his grin vanished and his young brow wrinkled as he asked himself who was the other man who had stopped so close to him, and had turned his gaze in the direction of 12A. What was his interest in the house, and why had he cursed softly when his watch was disturbed?

He had gone on down the street, and Tinker had seen nothing of him since; but he had little doubt that, like himself, the other lay concealed in the shelter of a dark area-way. He saw the plain-clothes man take a look at 12A, and move on down the street, evidently on his way to the rear.

Scarcely had he disappeared when Tinker heard further footsteps, and, once more craning his neck outwards, saw the man in the ulster coming up the street. His interest in 12A had driven him to leave his place of concealment, and move closer to the object of his gaze.

He did not stand so close to Tinker this time, and the lad could risk a little movement without fear of discovery. He made every effort to gain some idea of the man's features, but the brim of the soft hat held them effectually in shadow and made his attempt useless.

Just then, still another footfall sounded at the head of the street. The man in the ulster turned his head sharply and, with a smothered exclamation, turned and started along at a brisk pace. For a single moment Tinker hesitated, then he slipped forth from the area-way, and, after a cautious look around, started off. Looking ahead he saw that the newcomer in the street was a woman.

The man ahead passed her without turning, and when she got abreast of Tinker, the lad did likewise. The man in the ulster was his quarry for the moment, but, at the same time, he never dreamed that the woman he had just passed was also an actor in the little drama of interest playing round No. 12A.

Had he guessed for a moment that it was Mademoiselle Yvonne, and that she had come to Fulton Terrace for the express purpose of watching the house of mystery, he would have been tempted to let his quarry go and return to keep watch on her. But he didn't, so about the time Yvonne took up her station, Tinker was just turning out of the street on the trail of the man in the ulster.

A crawling taxi drew in close to the kerb, and Tinker saw his man hesitate as though he intended taking it. Then he made a negative gesture, and started on again at a brisk pace. Tinker heaved a sigh of relief. The taxi would have complicated matters.

From that point on, the chase led through street after street, until Knightsbridge was reached. There the man in the ulster paused in front of a huge shop and waited. Sauntering up, Tinker did likewise and, in the light cast from the shop windows, he saw that the man wore a heavy black beard.

At that moment a 'bus lumbered up and drew in to the kerb. Tinker's quarry jumped on to the rear platform, and made his way up to the roof. The lad followed, and managed to get a seat directly behind the other, just as the 'bus started with a jerk. Involuntarily, the man's hand went to his beard, and Tinker grunted softly as the gesture told him the beard was false.

Along Knightsbridge went the 'bus until it came to Hyde Park Corner, then down Piccadilly to Piccadilly Circus, and along Shaftesbury Avenue until New Oxford Street was reached. There Tinker's quarry rose and made his way down to the street, the lad close on his heels.

The man in the ulster walked briskly across until he came to the entrance of the Underground; there he entered, and when he bought a ticket for Cannon Street, Tinker was close behind with his money ready to purchase a ticket for the same point.

From that on until his quarry alighted at Cannon Street, it was easy work from Tinker's point of view. The man in the ulster sought a corner of the carriage and, leaning back, let his head sink on his chest. He may have been asleep, but Tinker did not think so.

At Cannon Street Station the chase led to the street, thence along to Great Tower Street, and past Tower Hill. From Tower Hill the man in the ulster turned his steps in the direction of the London Docks. He went along East Smithfield for some distance, finally turning down between a narrow lane of dark, silent warehouses.

Up to now it had not been difficult for Tinker to follow his man without creating suspicion for, from Cannon Street to Tower Hill, there had been a sufficient number of people abroad to render him unsuspicious. But now he realised he must exercise the greatest caution.

The heavy darkness made it necessary for him to keep fairly close to his quarry in order not to lose him in some one of the numerous turnings and alleys which led off on every side. Consequently, he was compelled to bring into play all the cleverness of which he was possessed.

From point to point, from corner to corner, from building to building he dodged, taking advantage of every shadowy spot to cover his movements. Twice the man ahead stopped as though he were listening, but on each occasion Tinker flattened himself against the wall of a black warehouse, and stood in rigid silence until the other started on again.

In this manner the chase led through a maze of turnings in the neighbourhood of the docks which, had Tinker not had a profoundly intimate knowledge of that part of the city, would have baffled him to find his way out again.

Steadily his quarry continued on until he reached the edge of a small canal, the waters of which appeared like a stream of ink. Along the edge of this he went for some five minutes, then once more he turned, and, for the third time, Tinker heard his footsteps pause. Hard on this came the sound of a door opening and closing. Then deep silence reigned.

Slowly and cautiously Tinker crept forward until a dark doorway loomed up ahead of him. He felt certain it was into this his quarry had disappeared, but, to make certain, he moved still closer and, crouching down, pressed his ear hard against the door. Almost at once he heard the sound of creaking inside, and put it down to the sound of the man making his way up an old staircase.

With infinite caution he lifted his hand and tried the latch. It lifted easily enough, but when he pressed the door refused to budge. His quarry had taken the precaution of bolting it after him. With a grunt of disappointment, Tinker drew back and took note of as much of his surroundings as he could make out in the darkness.

In front of him the building loomed dark and silent. The lower part was undoubtedly used as a warehouse, as was soon proved by a cursory examination of the iron-barred windows. From the fact that his quarry had ascended to the floor above, he figured the top was a loft, evidently let out as living quarters to some of the men who worked about the docks.

At that moment a gleam of light showed above him. Looking up he saw that a candle or lamp had been lighted in a room overhead and, even as he watched, a shadow passed across the window. Tinker took another careful survey of his surroundings, and, as his gaze took in a telephone pole near at hand, he breathed with satisfaction.

Stealthily he approached it and felt for a foothold or kneehold. There was none. Nor was the girth of the pole such that shinnying up it would be an easy or a quiet matter. Its top, disappearing in the darkness above, told him it was high, and that he would probably find no handhold or foothold until he had gone some feet past the necessary height which he figured would bring him close to, and just opposite, the window overhead from which the light shone.

But these difficulties did not deter him from his purpose. Had he given up in the face of things of that nature, Tinker would never have reached the position of responsibility and trust which he had reached with Sexton Blake.

For a few moments he pondered the situation, then found what he thought was a solution. Swiftly his hands went to his waist and he unbuckled his belt. It was of strong leather, with a heavy buckle, and in the course of its career had been used in many weird ways. More than once it had been a trusty friend in a tight corner, for there is hardly any better weapon at close quarters than a good belt with a weighty buckle.

This belt Tinker strapped loosely about his knees, leaving his limbs good play. Then, grasping the pole with both hands, he sprang upwards, his knees circling the pole as far as the spread of the belt would allow. He brought them in close until the belt was hard against the pole; then, resting his weight on the belt, he raised his arms and began to draw himself up.

Slowly but surely he progressed, first drawing himself upwards, then lifting his knees to rest upon the belt and raising his arms again. In this way he achieved his purpose both silently and without any great expenditure of breath.

Steadily he drew closer to the window overhead which was his objective. The frequent passing and repassing of the shadow told him his quarry was evidently pacing the room, and this assumption only made the lad more eager than ever to pierce the secret of the loft in the East End of London, where resided a man who had a more than ordinary interest in Fulton Terrace in the West End of London, and more particularly in No. 12A, where just about twenty-four hours before a terrible murder had been committed.

Even as he climbed, Tinker went over in his mind what few remarks Blake had dropped, and what he had heard at the inquest. Since his discovery that the man in the ulster could not be a plain clothes' detective, Tinker had been trying to reconcile him with one of the two mysterious personages who had been at No. 12A on the night of the murder.

He asked himself more than once if it could be the man who was there during the earlier part of the evening, or the man who had been surprised in the study by Sergeant Mullin and his men.

The fact that the man had kept his face so effectually concealed, had made it impossible for Tinker to gain any definite idea of his features, but he remembered the incident on the top of the 'bus when a violent lurch of the vehicle had caused the man to clutch at his beard. Now, in his own retreat, and as he would probably think, free from observation, Tinker hoped to see him with the mask off.

By this time the lad had climbed to within a foot of the window. Now he was up another six inches; now his head was level with the sill; and at last, another effort and his eyes could see into the room.

There was the window only the width of the pavement away from him; there was, as he had thoroughly expected, an old loft fitted up roughly as a place of habitation, and the figure of a man pacing up and down, up and down, up and down, with the monotonous regularity of a caged beast.

Nor was that all, for now the ulster was removed, and the beard lay on the table beside an empty bottle which formed, for the moment, a candlestick holding a flickering candle, the man's features were in full view, and as he took rapid note of them, Tinker tried to fit them to the butler's description of the man who had called on Gilbert Jefferson the evening before.

Certainly, the height was about the same, and the clothes were quite as rough as those described by the butler. Outwardly, the man might have seemed a wharf labourer, but something in the carriage of the head, something in the man's whole bearing —the unconscious air of authority, and the arrogant of face —told Tinker, though the garb and place of residence might be those of a dock labourer, the man upon whom he looked was no member of that great army.

His experience and the studies under Blake had taught him more than a little of the science of physiognomy, and, though he could not go so far as could Blake in his deductions of personality, and the indexing of any given human being in his class and probable occupation, still he could bring sufficient experience into play to prove that the man before him was a masquerader.

He knew it was improbable that the butler had been mistaken in his estimate of his master's caller. Old servants are more discerning than the average individual as regards class distinction, and Tinker knew a dozen little points of bearing and manner would enable the butler to judge correctly.

Assuming that to be so, it seemed hardly possible that the man upon whom he had now looked could be the same. Then, was it possible it was the man who had been surprised in the study by the police? That he could not tell; but had he been aware of the results of Blake's deductions on this point, he would have known that it could not be.

There seemed little of interest in the room itself. In one corner was a rough cot-bed, though even from where he was, Tinker could see the linen upon it was spotlessly clean. In the middle of the room was a rough deal table, upon which reposed the beard and the bottle already mentioned, as well as the remains of a meal.

Two chairs, and a small mirror hanging on the opposite wall, completed the furnishings as far as Tinker could see. In the far corner was a door.

The man inside was still pacing up and down, and, so far, showed no signs of stopping. That something was weighing heavily on his mind was evident from the depressed and worried look he wore, as well as the restless pacing to which his thoughts drove him.

But watching from a distance by no means filled Tinker's ideas of what the occasion demanded. Since he had begun to feel positive that the man was one of a very different class masquerading as a longshoreman, he had also begun to have an urgent desire to know the reason.

He wanted to know why the man had been at Fulton Terrace that evening. He wanted to know what his interest was in No. 12 A, where, only the evening before, a murder had been committed. He wanted to know why he was lodging in an old warehouse loft by the London Docks, and passing as a wharf labourer. And when he knew these things, he wanted to make for Baker Street at top speed with his report.

Those were his desires, and it is safe to say that when Tinker wanted to find out a thing very much, he did not spend much time figuring the risks attendant upon the acquisition of such knowledge, but went ahead to achieve his purpose. And so it was in this case.

Making up his mind that, like all buildings, the warehouse had a roof, and that, like a good many, it might have a skylight, he decided to investigate in order to find out if this were so. Gazing upwards, he could see a vague maze of wires overhead; beneath was the ground and a locked door.

Since he had climbed so high, he figured it was just as well to go higher, and see if any opening presented itself above. With this object in view, he once more began his ascent, using the belt as a grip and rest as he had done before.

About ten feet up he came to the first crossbar. There he sat long enough to slip the belt on his legs, and, buckling it once more about his waist, took another survey of his surroundings. A confusing array of crossbars broke the line above, and from them reached and stretched away a bewildering number of wires, invisible after a few feet, and looking as though the ends floated of their own accord.

These interested Tinker not in the least, but what caught his gaze, and held it, was a branching series of wires which left the third crossbar, and ran in the direction of the warehouse. A little thought told him these in all probability fed some building in an adjoining street, and that, as is often the case, the roof of the building had been utilised to support them.

Moving with great care, he drew himself up to the second crossbar, then to the third. Although the distance was not great, it was no easy matter, for so thick were the wires, and so dark the night, it needed all his ingenuity to crawl through them. Arrived at the third crossbar, he settled himself, and followed with his eyes the direction taken by the branching wires.

It was impossible to see in the dark whether they were attached to the roof of the warehouse or not, and, if not, Tinker knew they might pass so high above it that a drop from them would be highly dangerous in the dark. As far as he could figure, however, there was no other way of discovering whether the roof contained a skylight. So, finally deciding to risk the way which offered, he started on his journey.

Even in daylight, with one's destination in sight, and light to guide one's footsteps and handholds, it is no easy matter to cross an abyss by means of wires. Tightly though they may be strained, they give and swing to a heavy weight, and if they be strained too tightly, or badly joined, a snap may occur at any moment, and precipitate one into the abyss below. It was this daring journey which Tinker was attempting.

Placing his feet on a couple of wires which ran lowest, and were close together, he grasped another pair which ran higher, and, when he stood upright, were about the height of his waist. Another pair ran along about the height of his knees, and these he found convenient for leaning against, look behind, he started on his journey.

Inch by inch, foot by foot, he moved along, sliding first his hands to a new grip, then bringing his feet after to a point beneath where he held on.

He could now see that the roof was of a sloping description, and that the wires took a steady upward trend, indicating that if they were fastened to the roof, it was at the highest part.

After five long minutes, which seemed to him like hours, he looked down to see the edge of the roof, directly beneath him. It was hard to judge the exact distance, but he knew it could not be less than six feet. A drop to that sloping surface in the darkness was out of the question.

If he failed to grip the roof, or should slip, nothing could save him from being precipitated into the street beneath. Now the upward course of the wires was beginning to wear on him. His feet persisted in slipping back continually, and most of his weight, as well as his progress, now depended on his hands.

The way ahead looked terribly long, and the distance he had covered began to seem woefully short. But the memory of the man in the room below spurred him on to fresh efforts, and instead of letting himself slip back to the pole, he gritted his teeth and continued his course.

With maddening slowness the edge of the roof began to recede. It was impossible to see the top of it yet, but he consoled himself with the thought that it could not be far now. Then, just as he was contemplating the advisability of taking a rest, he looked ahead and saw it.

Gazing down, he could now see that the roof was only about four feet beneath him, proving that the wires must run close to the top. And so it was. Another yard, and he dared risk lowering himself until his feet touched the surface of the roof; then, using the wires to assist him, he drew himself along until he reached the saddle-back of the roof. To it the wires were attached by insulators barely six inches high, explaining why the roof had come nearer as he progressed.

As soon as he got his breath, Tinker began to look about him for signs of a skylight. His examination from the street had shown him that the warehouse only contained two floors— the ground floor, and the one comprising the loft where his quarry resided.

But by the light of the candle in the loft-room he had seen that the ceiling was flat, and as he now knew the roof to be of the sloping, saddle-back description, he also knew there must be some sort of a rough attic above the loft. Whether it was ever used, or whether it was even lighted by a skylight, remained yet to be proved.

Using his hands and knees as grips, he made his way along the roof until he had covered a good twenty feet. All the way he had been keeping a sharp look-out to right and left to see if any signs of a skylight showed in the surface, but nothing but the black roof had met his gaze. Turning cautiously, he made his way back and, crawling over the wires, started in the other direction.

He had covered less than three feet of his journey, when suddenly ahead, a little to his right, appeared the gleam of a light apparently shining through the very roof itself. Like a flash he was lying flat along the saddle-back, his body glued to the roof, watching intently.

For a moment the light wavered, then it disappeared, as suddenly as it had come. Tinker knew now that the roof did contain a skylight, and, not only that, but that someone, probably his quarry, was in the attic immediately beneath. At that moment a sound caught his ear.

First he heard a faint click, then followed a slow rubbing sound, and as he heard it, Tinker's pulses began to hammer madly. Whoever was in the attic beneath was opening the skylight. Was it for ventilation, or with the intention of coming to the roof? If the latter, had they heard him, and was that the reason for their coming?

As he asked himself the question, Tinker gazed ahead with every nerve tense. Nor was the answer long in coming. Against the darkness ahead he saw something appear. Steadily it grew and grew until he could make out the outlines of a man's head and shoulders. Someone was hoisting himself through the skylight to the roof.

For one desperate moment Tinker thought of retreat, but a moment's consideration told him such a course would be useless. The other would hear his slightest move, and, though the slope of the wires would make a quick, daring slide back to the pole a risky possibility, he had no fancy to be shot or precipitated to the street below by the other shaking him from the wires. And he knew such a plan would occur to the most stupid of pursuers.

Neither had he any fancy for a hostile meeting on the saddle-back of that dark roof. If it were his quarry, and if the latter were the cause of the murder at Fulton Terrace, Tinker knew exactly how desperate the encounter would be.

He could not retreat; he dared not advance. There was nothing to do but cling on and wait. He did manage to draw his revolver, and, with this clutched in one hand, he sat waiting.

All this time the other had been moving on his purpose. Tinker had seen his body come into view, and now he watched him as, bracing one foot against the edge of the skylight, he began to squirm up the sloping surface to the saddle-back. Tinker had heard the skylight close, and judged that wherever the other intended going, he evidently did not propose returning soon.

Tinker held his breath as the other reached the top of the roof and sat astride; then, as the figure began to move again, the lad gathered himself together for the meeting he felt could not now be avoided. But after a moment his brow wrinkled in puzzlement.

He was positive the other was moving steadily along the roof, yet he seemed to get no nearer. Then suddenly the truth burst upon Tinker. He was travelling in the opposite direction.

A wave of relief swept over the lad as he realised what was happening. So keyed up had he been, so anticipatory of a dramatic meeting, and perhaps a struggle to the death on that roof, that the reaction almost caused him to make a betrayal of his presence in the sharp intake of breath which he took. As it was, the figure ahead stopped as though listening, but Tinker crouched low, and after a moment the other resumed his course.

For a full two minutes Tinker lay motionless, watching the man ahead. He saw his outline grow more and more indistinct as it blended with the night, then, following that, he heard a soft scraping sound, and afterwards another noise. As far as he could judge, the man had slid down the sloping roof, and had entered another skylight.

A faint gleam of light far ahead convinced him that this was so; then it disappeared, and silence reigned once more. Though he had seen the outline of the man who had come through one skylight and disappeared through another, Tinker had, of course, been unable to see his features.

Consequently, he could not tell whether it were his quarry or not. But if it were, he realised he had an unique opportunity for pursuing his investigations in the loft-room over the warehouse. At any rate, since he had risked so much, he decided to go the limit and risk more.

With this intention, he once more began his progress along the roof until he came to a point opposite the skylight through which he had seen the man come. Taking a grip on the inverted V-shaped edge of the roof, he let his legs slide downwards until his feet rested against the edge of the skylight. Then he released his hold, and screwing about cautiously, worked his way round until he considered it safe to make a reach for the framework of the skylight with his hands.

He succeeded in grasping it, and once he had a solid hold it took him very few seconds to find the catch. After that it was the work of only a minute to discover that the skylight was unlocked and to lift it. Holding it up with one hand, he slipped first one leg and then the other over the edge, and let his feet dangle over the black abyss which yawned beneath.

Almost immediately one of his feet encountered something, which upon investigation proved to be a rope ladder; hanging from the skylight. On discovering this, Tinker acted at once. It was evident that, since the man he had seen had taken the trouble to secure a rope ladder, he must make frequent use of the skylight as a means of exit and ingress.

He racked his brains, wondering what the other's purpose could be, but, realising that the solution of that must come after the present problem, he put it from his mind.

He grasped the framework of the skylight with one hand, and holding the sash up with the other, placed both feet on the rope ladder. Then he felt for the next cross rope, and, as he descended to it, let the skylight come down. A moment later it was closed, and, for good or ill, he was cautiously descending the ladder into the blackness beneath.

Much sooner than he expected his feet encountered the floor, and releasing his hold on the ladder he stood rigid, listening. Not a sound broke the stillness. He felt cautiously in his pocket, and, after fumbling for a moment, drew out his pocket torch. Pressing the switch, he cast the circle of light about him.

He found himself, as he had half expected, in a rough attic room of small dimensions. Beyond the rope ladder which hung from the skylight there was absolutely nothing in the room. The floor in one corner was broken by a hole, through which projected a ladder, and towards this Tinker softly made his way.

Standing at the edge, he cast the light through, revealing a bare passage beneath, and, bending he could discern a door at the end. That decided him. Extinguishing the light, he slipped it back into his pocket, and gripped the uprights of the ladder, then, wrapping his legs about it, he slid softly down, fireman fashion.

Arrived at the bottom he again stood listening. Still silence reigned, and from beneath the door at the end of the passage came no gleam of light. He wondered if it were the loft-room into which he had looked from the telephone pole, and he wondered if he would find it empty, or occupied by the man who had so excited his curiosity.

He crept forward step by step until his fingers encountered the door itself, then feeling for the handle he turned it and pressed gently. The door swung inwards without the slightest resistance, and still gripping his revolver in one hand Tinker slipped through into the room.

For a moment he stood just inside the door. But if the room contained an occupant, no sound indicated the fact. Tinker risked the use of his pocket light again, and at the first flash saw he was indeed in the room into which he had looked from outside.

He saw, moreover, that it was deserted, and that the beard which had reposed on the table had disappeared. Everything else was exactly as it had been, except the candle was not to be seen.

One thing Tinker did notice which he had not seen before. That was a big iron chest against the wall beneath the window. From where he had looked into the room it had, naturally, been out of his line of vision.

A further glance about the room told him that if the barely-furnished place held any secret, that secret would only be in the iron box, so towards this he crept. When he reached it he knelt down and examined the lock. He recognised it as an old one, and one not difficult to force, providing he were given a little time.

Before attempting it, he extinguished the light again, and sat listening, then, deciding to risk it, he pressed the switch and laid the torch on the floor. That done, he acted swiftly.

Drawing from his pocket a steel instrument which looked like a shining metal spider, and of which Blake had taught him the use, he placed two of the metal "feelers" in the keyhole, and went to work. For a good five minutes he worked patiently, turning, twisting, and pressing in his search for the right position. At the end of that time he heard a click, and, knew the barricade had been passed.

Withdrawing the instrument, he replaced it in his pocket, and laid hold of the lid. He lifted it up cautiously, and was greeted by the sight of a shallow tray, in which reposed a medley of articles. Tinker let the lid back until it rested against the wall, then his eager hands went towards the tray.

Swiftly, but thoroughly, he examined the contents. In one corner lay a sealed envelope with no writing on it. This he thrust aside for the moment. Next he came upon a small box, which on being opened revealed a ring set with a large solitaire diamond, a scarf-pin, set with a big pearl.

Instinctively Tinker turned the watch over, and the letters which formed the monogram on the back seemed to burn themselves into his brain. There were only two, but how they made his heart leap as he read them —and what a host of meaning they spelled to him! "G. J." were the initials he saw.

Had he really found the retreat of the murderer of Gilbert Jefferson, and was he actually handling the dead man's watch, torn from him by the hands of the man who had done the deed? He asked himself that as he replaced the watch and examined the other articles in the tray.

A few sheets of paper next met his gaze, and, picking them up, he was dumbfounded to see that they each and all bore exactly the same lines written upon them. Nor was his amazement lessened when, on reading them closely, he discovered them to be word for word copies of the half-finished letter which had been found on the desk in front of the murdered man at No. 12A, Fulton Terrace.

And that was not all. Each bit of writing broke off at the same word, and on each paper was an irregular line, as though a pen had fallen and rolled across them. What did it mean?

Acting on impulse, Tinker folded them up and stuffed them in his pocket. A second impulse drove him to do the same with the box containing the ring, pin, and watch. Then, after satisfying himself that the rest of the contents of the tray were of an unimportant nature, he lifted it out in order to see what might be beneath.

As he did so a startled gasp of amazement fell from his lips, and the tray slid, with a loud crash, to the floor. And well might his control have been momentarily upset, for in the bottom of the iron box was a great heap of golden sovereigns, which must have contained thousands of pieces!

It was stupefying, unbelievable, dazzling! And even ere Tinker had recovered his self-possession a sharp hiss sounded behind him.

With another startled gasp, he turned to see the man he had followed standing in the doorway, gazing at him over the barrel of a steadily-held automatic pistol.

Blake had gone barely half a dozen steps when suddenly he was blinded by the glare of a powerful light full in his eyes. He stepped back involuntarily, and raised a hand to shield his eyes. *(Chapter 8.)*

The whole street seemed to rise up in a great blinding flash of
light, to the accompaniment of a terrific explosion. (*Chapter 8.*)

To return to Blake. After his startling discovery of the third black skull on his desk immediately following the departure of Hammerton Palmer, he began to readjust several of his ideas. Vague suspicions and tentative theories which he had held before, and which he had kept securely locked in his own breast, now began to take a more definite form.

As to the footprints at the rear of No. 12A, Fulton Terrace, and what they spelled to him; the strange will of Gilbert Jefferson, and the still stranger incident of the twenty thousand pounds in gold; the desperate financial condition seven months before of Gilbert Jefferson, and his subsequent rapid rise to a credit balance; the fact that Hammerton Palmer seemed intimately connected with that period of time, and that by the terms of the will the financier was not to suffer, no matter what payments had to be met by the estate; the murdered man himself, and the disfigurement which had been caused by the powerful acid; and the strange incident of the three ebony skulls with the grinning ivory teeth, Blake had thought a good deal.

But not even Tinker knew what that puzzling array of facts set in motion in Blake's mind. Nor did he even permit himself as yet to write down in his private notebook the possibilities they suggested to him. Before forming such definite theories as that, he must put several things to the test, and the imminent danger which that third black skull spelled inspired him to lose no time.

Pondering over the conversation he had had on the 'phone with Alice Jefferson just previous to Hammerton Palmer's call upon him, and following a trend of thought suggested by the third black skull, Blake decided to make a further visit to Fulton Terrace without delay. He had not seen Formby Mott, the lawyer, since the afternoon, and, consequently, knew nothing of the appearance of Mademoiselle Yvonne at the offices of the Jefferson Silk Company, and of the indications that a battle seemed imminent between her and Hammerton Palmer for the control of the company.

In fact, he did not even know Yvonne was a shareholder in the company, nor had he any knowledge of the paper which Hammerton Palmer claimed to possess, and which, he said, contained a direct injunction to Alice Jefferson from her uncle to be guided by Palmer in all her dealings with the stock of the Jefferson Silk Company.

Those things he was to discover later, so it was with an idea of following up the facts of which he already had cognisance that he donned his coat and hat immediately after dinner, and set out for Fulton Terrace.

Realising that No. 12A would undoubtedly be under surveillance by Inspector Thomas's man as well as by Tinker, and from his latest readings of certain happenings, that it was just possible other parties might take an interest in the terrace as well, Blake decided to go by 'bus as far as Knightsbridge, and to walk from there.

With this idea in view he set off at a brisk walk for Oxford Street. Now at night, although a very orderly thoroughfare, Baker Street is quiet, and in some places, dark. During his long career Blake had often found the shadowy spots of the street an asset, as well as an element of danger. More than once had they served as a place of concealment while he watched some individual who showed a more than ordinary interest in Blake's house, and more than once had some deadly assault been precipitated upon him from them.

Yet, even though he had read in the third black skull a murderous threat, and though he knew there were hidden elements of menace at work, he did not anticipate a move against him immediately. Consequently his glances to right and left, as he walked along, were no more piercing than usual.

He had covered perhaps half the distance to Portman Square, without passing half a dozen people altogether. Busy as he was with his thoughts he gave them little heed, nor did he bestow more than a cursory glance upon the occasional motor or taxi which passed. Therefore, when he had reached this distance, the sound of a slowly approaching motor behind him did not even cause him to turn his head.

Then something happened so swiftly and suddenly that he was totally unable to gain any coherent idea of what it was. He was conscious of a sudden roar from the motor as it was jerked into the high speed, and he caught a momentary glimpse of it as it flew past him. Then the whole street seemed to rise up in a great blinding flash of light to hurl itself upon him, to the accompaniment of a terrific explosion; the buildings seemed to leap at him as though to crush him, and upon a wave of light and confusion Blake was borne into oblivion.

His next conscious thought was to realise that he was sitting on the pavement with a crowd about him, and two blue-uniformed constables forcing brandy down his throat; he endeavoured to grasp what was being said.

"You have had a close shave, sir," one of them was saying, "Another two inches and you would have been crushed to powder. Look here, sir. See this granite pillar? It was toppled over here and fell not two inches from your ear, and it weighs over a ton. How do you feel now, sir?"

Blake felt himself for broken bones, but deciding that there were none, he clambered to his feet with the assistance of the constables.

"I don't think that there is anything seriously wrong," he smiled wanly. "I quite see that I had a miraculous escape. I presume it was one of the uprights of that iron fence which has been twisted so artistically which struck me."

"Yes, sir, and at the same time drove you forward enough to be the means of saving your life."

"But what has happened, officer? I have a confused notion that there was a terrific explosion, and that is about all."

"You have it right, sir. We have a witness here who saw it all. He was coming along some distance behind you. He says a powerful motor drove past him slowly until it got close to you. At that moment his attention was particularly attracted to it, owing to the fact that the driver threw on the high speed with great suddenness.

"As he looked, he saw a man in the tonneau rise and hurl something at you; then the car shot on, and the explosion occurred when the bomb struck. You can see how powerful it was and what an escape you had, sir.

"And now, if you will let me have your name and address, and tell us if you have any suspicions as to who could be the perpetrators, we will make the report and start a search for the car."

Blake leaned back against the twisted iron fence and drew out a cigarette.

"I'll tell you my name, officer," he said smiling. "It is Sexton Blake."

"Good heavens!"

As he made the exclamation the constable stepped forward and peered into Blake's face.

"By thunder, so it is," he said, turning to his fellow officer.

The small crowd murmured and pressed closer, endeavouring to get a nearer view of the great detective, who now loomed a hundred times more important in their eyes since they knew his identity.

Blake lifted his hand.

"Listen, officer," he said. "There is no doubt but that a desperate and deliberate attempt was made upon my life. I fancy the throwing of the bomb and the starting of the car into high speed, were not perfectly timed, otherwise not even the blow from the iron picket would have saved me.

"I have an idea, also, that I may know the source of the attack, but at present I do not care to press the matter. No good can come of it, but I assure you, if the time does come when a move will be of use, I shall let you know. There are a good many people, you know, who would give a great deal to see me dead."

And with this Blake made his escape. He was compelled to walk slowly at first, for his head ached violently and his brain a till swam, but with each step he grew steadier under the cool night air, and by the time he finally turned into Oxford Street, he was feeling a good deal better.

He found a 'bus which would take him to his destination, and sought the top. Once he was ensconced in a seat he gave his thoughts to the outrage which had just been attempted. He realised full well how deliberate had been the attempt upon his life, and, as he had told the policeman, it was not hard for him to guess where it had emanated.

He put it down without hesitation to an attempt to carry out the sentence of death which had been pronounced upon him. Now he knew his deductions on that point were correct, and yet he marvelled at the boldness of the mysterious individuals who seemed represented by Hammerton Palmer, the financier.

How secure they must feel; how utterly confident of immunity must Palmer be to work so openly. A few hours before he had been but a casual factor in the case; now, of his own volition, he had stepped out into the open, had thrown down the gauntlet and, if Blake's deductions were correct, had followed up his challenge by a dastardly attempt on Blake's life. Proof that every move in the case was being watched and combated.

Evidently they had made up their minds that the murder at No. 12A, Fulton Terrace was not to be solved if they could prevent it, and the murderous attempt that night showed what they considered the most dangerous element in their plans. That was Sexton Blake.

On arriving at Knightsbridge, Blake descended from the 'bus and started on foot towards Fulton Terrace. It was when he arrived, there and ascended the steps that Tinker saw him.

As always, he made some sign when he knew Tinker to be about which would tell the lad that he was on the spot.

His ring was answered promptly, and old Parker, the butler, admitted him. Before asking for Miss Jefferson he spoke to Parker.

"Before you call your mistress, Parker," he said, "I wish to have a word with you. Come along to the study. I will await her there."

He passed down the hall, and, once inside, signed to the butler to close the door.

"Now then, Parker," he said quietly, "I want you to cast your mind back over several months. I want you to go over your master's movements carefully, and be prepared to answer one or two questions with certainty. Firstly, was it your master's custom to go out frequently in the evening?"

"No sir. He rarely went out after dinner."

"Did he receive many friends here?"

"No sir. He was a man, if I might say so, who kept mostly to himself."

"Then you recall nothing regarding his goings and comings which struck you as being out of the ordinary?"

The old butler shifted and looked down.

"I'll tell you something, sir. It didn't strike me as having any bearing on his death, and being his own private movements, I said nothing of it. For some months the master had made it a habit to go out regularly on the last evening of the month. If that day fell on the thirtieth he went that evening; if it fell on the thirty-first, that was the night he went.

"Where he went, or on what business he was bound, I don't know, sir; but I couldn't help noticing that the next morning after he was always very cheerful —in fact, quite elated, if I may say so, sir. That is, every time except the last."

"Ah! What was his mental condition after the last time, Parker?"

"The next morning he was very much depressed, sir. He ate little, and left earlier than usual for his office. That was about ten days ago, sir, and I must say that from that time to his death, his movements were irregular.

"He went out several evenings running, and straight up to the day of his death was in the same depressed condition. I did not connect it with the —the murder, sir. I put it down to something else."

"What did you put it down to, Parker?"

"Well, sir, I couldn't help but know that the master had been dealing heavily on the Stock Exchange. Then he told me himself one morning, several months ago, that he was done with it. His regular evening journeys began after that, and I thought, sir, he had perhaps joined a gaming club where they might play for high stakes. I put down his cheerful manner that he had won, and after the last time, I thought perhaps he had lost heavily."

"You are a very discerning fellow, Parker, and your information is of more importance than you know. Now, before you call Miss Jefferson, will you make me a promise?"

"Yes, sir."

"Good! I want you to promise that you will breathe not a word of what you have told me to a soul —not even to Miss Jefferson. Can I depend on you for that? Very well, I trust you to observe that. Now call your mistress, please."

Parker departed on his errand and a few moments later Alice appeared. One look at her face told Blake she was in a highly nervous state, and her first words convinced him that developments of some kind had taken place since he had been there in the afternoon.

"Oh, Mr. Blake!" she cried, "I am so glad you have come. I am so upset and so troubled that I don't know which way to turn."

"Keep your nerve, Miss Jefferson," answered Blake, soothingly, leading her to a chair, and taking the one opposite her. "Things will come out all right, don't worry. Now then, I can see something has happened since I was here this afternoon. Supposing you tell me quietly and calmly just what it is. Then I can help you."

"I feel as if I were in a sinister maze which will sweep me down, as it has swept my uncle down, Mr. Blake. I feel that people are all about me, and that a dozen eyes are watching my every movement. And, worse than all, I think I have got to ask you to abandon your work on the case."

"Yes? Why, Miss Jefferson?"

For answer she thrust her hand inside her blouse and drew out two letters. One of them she handed to Blake.

"That came to-night, Mr. Blake. Will you read it, please?"

Blake studied the envelope carefully before drawing out what it contained. He saw that it was typewritten, and had been posted in the East End at 3.30 that afternoon. Then he drew out the contents, which consisted of another envelope with a sheet of paper wrapped about it. He unfolded the paper first and read it. It was undated and unsigned, and had been typewritten, as had the outer envelope.

It said:

"To Miss Alice Jefferson.

"Dear Madam,—Enclosed you will find a sealed envelope which was left for safekeeping with the writer by your late uncle. His instructions were that in the case of his death by natural means or otherwise, it should be forwarded to you.

"Having read of his death in the papers I am sending it as per his instructions."

That was absolutely everything the sheet of paper contained. Next Blake examined the envelope which had been enclosed in the larger one. He saw that it was addressed in ink to "Miss Alice Jefferson."

Underneath was written:

"To be forwarded to her only in the event of my death," and there followed the initials "G. J."

Drawing out the enclosure, Blake found it to be another single sheet of paper, folded in three, and containing a few lines written in the same handwriting, which was on the envelope, handwriting which he had already recognised as being the same as he had seen on the half-written note found on the desk in front of the murdered man. Unfolding the paper he read what, it contained. Like the other it was brief and almost curt in tone. It said:

"My dear Niece—

"If you ever read these lines, it will be because you know I am dead. In my will I have provided for you as I always intended to provide for the child of my dear brother. I have left you sole mistress of your own affairs, and have created no hampering restrictions.

"By my affection for you and yours for me I charge you to carry out this my last request. It is this:

"In the case of my death occurring at any time through means which appear other than natural, I charge you to take no steps to investigate the reason. If such a thing should occur, receive the police and put no obstacles in their way, but under no circumstances go out of your way to assist them.

"Above all, do not engage any private investigator. This I wish to impress upon you most emphatically, if it happens that you have taken such steps before the receipt of this, dismiss him at once. I count on you not to fail. Let me rest in peace.

"Your affectionate uncle—Gilbert Jefferson."

Blake folded up the note and returned it to its envelope thoughtfully.

"There is no doubt in your mind that this was written by your uncle, I suppose?" he said, after a short pause.

"None at all, Mr. Blake. Both the writing and manner of phrasing are his."

"I see. Then there appears to be nothing for you to do but to release me from the case, Miss Jefferson. It appears from several points which have developed, that your uncle not only anticipated death, but that he thought it possible it might be of a violent nature. Though he may have wished investigations not to be made, his desire can hardly stop the police inquiry, but, of course, that does not prevent you from stopping all private inquiry."

"I know, Mr. Blake. I feel in my heart that no efforts should be spared to bring the perpetrators of the crime to justice, yet what can I do but follow his instructions? All he gave me are so plain I cannot pretend to misunderstand them."

"Quite right," responded Blake. "Since you feel that way about it, I should be the last person in the world to endeavour to persuade you to do otherwise. But before I go, will you tell me if anything else has developed?"

"Yes. Firstly I received another letter to-night. It is from Mr. Palmer. He must have written it shortly after leaving here to-day. Would you care to read it?"

"If I may."

She handed over the second letter to him, and with barely a glance at the envelope Blake drew out the enclosure. It was headed with Hammerton Palmer's name and business address, and was as follows:

"Dear Miss Jefferson,

"I must ask you to forgive my writing you so soon about business matters, but it is necessary for your own good that I do so.

"After leaving you this afternoon I called at the offices of the Jefferson Silk Company. Though probate of your uncle's will has not yet been obtained, I took it upon myself to instruct the secretary of the company to call a meeting of the shareholders. I considered this advisable in view of the manner of your uncle's death, and that in the interests of the company and the shareholders, a statement of the present condition of the company should be made out.

"Since then I have received a telephone message from the secretary. He tells me that almost immediately after my departure a large shareholder in the company called and countermanded my instructions. He said the shareholder was fully aware of the terms of your late uncle's will and considered that by it she (it is a woman) now became the individual controlling interest in the firm.

"Technically that is true, but a document made out by your uncle at the time I assisted him financially, alters this condition and leaves the control in my hands, providing you follow his wishes. This document I have in my possession and shall be pleased to submit at any time for your inspection.

"In a few words, it is a paper duly signed and witnessed charging you to be guided by me in your dealings with the Jefferson Silk Company. In other words, to vote your shares with mine.

"A few moments' consideration will show you that our mutual interests make this a wise thing, and I venture to say my knowledge of business and finance will suffice to protect your interests and my own. You must see the danger to yourself in allowing the control of the company to pass into other hands. It would mean that the business your late uncle spent his life upon would become the shuttlecock of strangers. In two words, we must stand together.

"Can I depend on you to resist all offers from other interests, to turn a deaf ear to all persuasion, and to stand shoulder to shoulder with me in this thing?

"Sincerely yours —Hammerton Palmer."

Blake read the letter over a second time, then he returned it to its envelope. That done he held it carelessly in his hand and glanced at the signature.

In his investigations, Blake had found it necessary to be on expert on many subjects, and not least amongst those subjects was the modern business marvel, the typewriter.

An exhaustive study of every make and model, and a thorough comparison of all the types used, had taught him one thing, that though every machine may be built with rigid exactitude according to plans, and though each and every part may be cut according to measurements, when they are all assembled they created machines each and every one of which attains its own individuality.

Take two machines of the same model and made on the same day from exactly similar parts. Use them for a month, and in that time the work turned out by each, though similar in the main, contains a hundred differences when examined closely.

A letter here may be out of alignment in one which is true in the other; part of a letter or sign may be worn in one and still perfect in the other. These are only examples of the many differences which show under expert examination.

And now, when he applied this knowledge to the two envelopes which had been addressed in type to Alice Jefferson that day, even a superficial glance showed Blake that there was a remarkable similarity in the addresses.

Both were pale blue in colour, both occupied about the same position on the envelope, and both had a strange air of relationship. But this superficial likeness was by no means all. The chief point of similarity between them was the letter "J" in the name Jefferson.

In each address the top of the letter sloped decidedly to the right as though the type bar on the machine had been slightly bent. Furthermore, every letter "e" on both envelopes showed a similar peculiarity in that all were blurred in identically the same manner.

To add to the likeness the capital A in No. 12A had the right leg of the A missing in each. The mathematical possibility that such identical peculiarities could occur in two different machines was a ratio of so many millions to one, that Blake knew it to be an utter impossibility. There were not enough machines in the world to provide the necessary number to supply the possibility.

Consequently he felt not only safe in assuming that each envelope had been addressed on the same machine, but was as certain of it as though he had himself witnessed the act.

He said nothing to Alice about this new piece of information, for she was under the impression he would do no more on the case after that night, and, though Blake had not the faintest intention of giving it up, he felt it was a good thing in more ways than one that she should continue to think so. He handed back the second letter without comment, then he spoke:

"You intimated that something else had occurred, I think?"

"Yes, Mr. Blake. It is this. When I went to my room after dinner, to lie down, I found it impossible to compose myself, so I got up again and sat at the window. I drew aside the curtains and lifted the window in order to get the air.

"As my room was in darkness I could sit in the shadow and look out without being seen. I had been there for less than fifteen minutes when something happened which attracted my attention. It was a lad who came down the street and stopped near the house.

"He seemed to survey it carefully, and was just moving on when he was joined by another lad. After a few moment's conversation the second boy departed, and I saw him no more. But the first one only went as far as a dark area-way and there he remained in the shadow.

"Almost immediately a man in a long ulster came down the street. He also stopped and looked across at the house and, although he stood close to the area-way where the lad lay concealed, he apparently did not see him. Suddenly the man in the ulster turned and walked on down the street. At the same moment the figure of another man came in sight, and I did not doubt that it was his appearance which had caused the other to move.

"The newcomer came down this side of the street, and looking out of the window, I could see that he also seemed to take an interest in the house as he passed. It may have been solely due to the awful tragedy which had occurred here. I do not know. At any rate, no sooner had he passed on than the man in the ulster again appeared and resumed his scrutiny.

"Just then another man came in sight, and ascended the steps. Now I know that it was you. When you had been admitted I rose with the intention of coming down at once, when a movement of the man in the ulster attracted my attention.

"He turned and started up the street, and no sooner had he done so than the lad who had lain concealed in the area-way stole out and followed after. On the way they passed a woman who had just turned into the street, and I calculated it was her appearance which had driven the man in the ulster from his post the second time.

"As he and the lad turned out of the street I glanced at her casually. I thought she could only be someone who lived in the street, and all the time I was watching her I was wondering who that man in the ulster could be, and what was his purpose.

"Then, suddenly, my attention became riveted on the woman. She had passed on until she came to a dark corner which is almost opposite here. There she stopped, and though she stood in the shadow, I could see she was watching this house. She was still there when I came down, and as far as I know may be there yet."

With a single, swift movement Blake was on his feet.

"I wish you had told me this when you first came down, Miss Jefferson. Do you mind letting me have a look at the Street from the window of your room?"

"Not at all, Mr. Blake. Will you come now?"

She rose and led the way. In the hall stood Parker, the butler, and with a brief motion of the hand Blake signed for him to follow them. And as they hurried up the stairs, neither Alice Jefferson nor Blake recalled that less than twenty minutes before he had practically been dismissed from the case.

How little she dreamed what an important element in Blake's mind was the introduction of a woman's interest in No. 12A. Neither she, nor the police, nor, in fact, a single soul knew what those footprints at the rear had spelled to him.

Where the police were under the impression that two men had visited the Jefferson house on the night of the murder, and were searching for two men, Blake was searching for one man.

The second, in his mind, was either a misshapen man or a woman, and the latter had fitted the results of his deductions more perfectly than anything else.

Though the note which had been handed to the boy in Knightsbridge formed a faint clue to the man who had visited Gilbert Jefferson earlier in the evening, there was absolutely nothing but those footprints leading from and back to the rear wall to form any clue to the identity of the visitor who had been surprised in the study by the police.

He (or she, as Blake figured a possibility) had utterly disappeared from the moment the waiting car had torn off down the street, and certainly it had left no traces of its movement. Consequently, no sooner had he heard from Alice Jefferson's lips that a woman had appeared and had taken an interest in No. 12A, than his own interest had leaped to fever heat.

On arriving at Alice Jefferson's room, Blake signed to the butler to close the door, and, leaving both him and Alice standing near it, he strode towards the window.

Cautiously drawing aside the curtains, he peered out. The street seemed utterly deserted. Not a foot-fall broke its silence, and only a few lights were visible. His eyes at once sought the dark corner mentioned by Alice Jefferson, and he strained them eagerly in an attempt to pierce its shadows. At first he thought he had been too late, and that whoever had stood there watching No. 12A had given up their vigil and had left.

But after a few minutes, when his eyes became more accustomed to the gloom, bethought he could make out something greyish against the darker background of the wall. He watched it intently for some moments, becoming more convinced than ever that he was right.

Then suddenly it moved, and he knew he had made no mistake. Someone was standing in the shadow of that dark corner watching the house where the murder had occurred.

Was it still the woman whom Alice Jefferson had seen? If it were, he meant to know more of her before that night was out, if such a thing were possible.

Rising softly, Blake let the curtains fall back into place, and made his way back to the two by the door,

"It is all right, Miss Jefferson," he said, "I have seen what you spoke of, but I don't think you need feel at all nervous. You know, of course, that the police are keeping a surveillance of the house, and nothing can harm you. Now I think I shall go. Do you object to Parker letting me out the back way?"

"Certainly not, Mr. Blake. Do you wish to leave without being observed?"

"Exactly."

As he spoke, Blake opened the door and held out his hand.

"You need not bother to come down, Miss Jefferson. You are tired, and I should advise you to try to get some rest. Goodnight."

With that he turned and, followed by the butler, made his way downstairs. When he reached the hall he turned to Parker.

"I think, Parker," he said, "I shall leave by the basement window which we examined this afternoon. You can close it after me."

"Very well, sir."

"And Parker."

"Yes, sir."

"Don't forget our little secret regarding your master's depressed condition and irregular movements just before the tragedy here."

"No, sir."

They made their way down to the basement, and along to the disused room. There Blake softly pushed back the catch, and with a whispered "Good-night" to the butler, crawled through. He stood motionless for a moment until he heard the window close behind him, then he started forward.

He had gone barely half a dozen steps when suddenly he was blinded by the glare of a powerful light full in his eyes. He stepped back involuntarily, and raised a hand to shield his eyes. He had by no means forgotten the attempt on his life such a short time before, and he had no fancy for a second experience of that nature the same night.

Then there flashed through his mind the thought that Inspector Thomas would be almost sure to have a man on watch at the rear of the house, and with this thought he spoke.

"If you will kindly take that light out of my eyes, I shall he greatly obliged, my friend," he said coolly.

For a moment it wavered, then it turned on one side, and a moment later he could make out the figure of a man just ahead of him.

"Who are you," came a gruff voice, "and what are you doing here?"

"I might ask you the same question," answered Blake, "but I won't. Instead, I will tell you who you are. You are an extremely worthy plain-clothes detective, sent here by Inspector Thomas, and who I can see is doing his duty in a thorough manner."

An astonished grunt told Blake he had struck the truth, and he smiled as the light was once more flashed into his eyes.

"H'm!" came the voice again. "I might have guessed. So it's you, is it, Mr. Blake?"

"Right first time," said Blake; "but please take that light away, it is blinding,"

The plain clothes' man removed the light, and Blake stepped close to him, peering into his face.

"It is you, is it, Manning? I rather thought the inspector would have somebody on the job. Did he tell you I was on the case?"

"No, he didn't, Mr. Blake; but I found it out when I got here."

"Ah! How?"

"I ran into a lad watching the rear of the place, and found it was the young lad your boy Tinker uses occasionally. He told me Tinker was in front."

"That was Tim," said Blake. "Where is he now?"

"I don't know. He left about twenty minutes ago to report to Tinker in front as they had arranged, and he hasn't come back."

"That is odd," said Blake slowly.

For a moment he stood in thought. He remembered what Alice Jefferson had said about the man in the ulster being followed out of the street by a lad. He had no doubts, either then or now, that it was Tinker. But she had made no mention of the other lad appearing after he had first parted from Tinker.

Computing the time, he figured that from what the plain clothes' man had said, Tim would have been making his way round to the front just about the time Alice Jefferson was in the library talking to him (Blake).

If that were the case, he would find Tinker gone, and, perhaps by arrangement with Tinker, he had taken up the latter's watch in front. Then, it that were so, he must have spotted the woman who was standing at the corner on the opposite side of the street from No. 12A.

Arriving at this conclusion, he turned to the plain-clothes' man.

"I am going now, Manning. If Tim should appear, will you tell him, please, to come on to Baker Street. I am not on the case any more."

"Not on the case, Mr. Blake?" exclaimed the other.

"No; Miss Jefferson has decided to leave all the investigations to the police."

"I am a bit sorry to hear that, sir. It doesn't look like an easy case."

"Nor is it, Manning. I think you will have your hands full. Good-night, and good luck to you."

With that Blake started on. Climbing over the fence, he made his way down the lane until he came to the street which led off at right angles to Fulton Terrace. Up this he turned and, taking the precaution to pull his hat well down over his eyes, and to turn up his collar, he started along.

He kept a sharp lookout for the dark corner opposite No. 12A, and when he reached it, looked sharply to see if the woman was still there on watch. A mere glance assured him that the corner was deserted, and that the shadows hid nothing but a few fallen leaves.

He glanced sharply up the side street which led from it. Not a sign. He then looked up and down the terrace, but it, too, was utterly deserted. A scrutiny of No. 12A told him no one was lurking there. Then what had become of the woman? Perhaps Tim would know.

Striding along, Blake paused under a light, and stopping, drew out a cigar. He then took out his matches and three flared up before he succeeded in lighting the weed.

If either Tinker or Tim were on watch, he knew the signal of the three matches would bring them up at once, for in Blake's signal code that particular one was marked "Urgent! Approach at once for fresh instructions."

He waited a full minute; but not a sign did he see of either lad. Again he made the signal, and again he waited, but nothing but the dreary moaning of the night wind answered him. And he knew now that Tinker was gone, that the woman who had stood in the shadow was gone, and that Tim was gone, too.

"Then in Heaven's name who was the man who was murdered?" Graves cried, and Blake had barely time to spring towards him and catch him as he crumpled up in a heap on the floor." (Chapter 9.)

"Oh! Oh! Oh!" The short, sharp gasps came from Yvonne's innermost being as she listened to Blake's slow, torturing words. (*Chapter 9.*)

THOUGH neither Tinker nor Tim had answered his twice-repeated signal, Blake did not make the mistake of risking a third, and thus arousing undue attention to himself. His theories had become advanced enough by now for him to realise that it was quite possible No. 12A might be an object of interest to more people than himself and the police.

The mysterious man in the ulster whom Tinker had apparently followed might well be a scout of Hammerton Palmer's; for, be it known, that since his interview with that influential gentleman, Blake had formed a theory which, though gigantic and stupendous in its bearing, fitted the frame of his theory in a marvellous manner.

It was no mushroom figment of the imagination, but the outgrowth of all the thought he had devoted, not only to the case in hand, but to those mysterious murders about which Inspector Thomas had more than once sought his assistance. It was, in a word, a result of his years of training and experience, and the point now was to steer the course of events so that they would lead him to a definite lane of evidence.

Then, and not till then, could he test the truth of his theory, and, if it were proved, to lay his hands on the persons who loomed in his mind as the cause.

He realised little good could come from remaining in Fulton Terrace. Several interesting things seemed to have happened there that evening, and he figured philosophically that Tinker would probably return to Baker Street with a report regarding the man in the ulster, and that if Tim had had the initiative to follow the mysterious woman, he would probably follow Tinker's example.

Therefore, the course of events seemed to indicate that his next move was to return to Baker Street and wait. Besides, he had a very keen desire to put more thought on what he had discovered from Alice Jefferson that evening —namely, the two letters which she had received —the one containing such an obviously anxious appeal from Hammerton Palmer for her co-operation, and the other a curt command from her uncle, telling her on no account to push forward inquiries as to the cause of his death, should such a thing occur.

And, strangely enough, both had been addressed upon the same machine. In truth, there was much food for thought in that.

His own experience a little earlier in the evening told him his safest means of reaching home was by taxi; so, on reaching the larger thoroughfare off which Fulton Terrace led, he hailed one which was crawling along near the kerb and, giving his address, climbed in and sank back in the corner.

He saw nothing of a suspicious nature when he reached Baker Street. A few loiterers still hung about gazing at the wreckage caused by the bomb, and a policeman was on duty at the spot. In front of his own house everything appeared perfectly normal and quiet. No lights showed, so Blake judged neither of the lads had yet returned to report.

On entering the consulting-room he saw that this was indeed the case. As usual, Blake's glance went first towards the desk to see if any letters had arrived during his absence. On the big blotting-pad reposed just one. It bore no stamp, and was addressed in a flowing hand. The fact of his name only being on the envelope, was a proof that it had been delivered by hand, and that the messenger had received verbal instructions as to the address.

Blake lifted it up, and after his usual scrutiny of the envelope, ripped it open. Inside was a single folded sheet of paper. This he drew out and unfolded. Then he read it.

It was a masterpiece of curtness. It said simply;

"We failed by inches only. The next time we will get you."

For a signature it had a small roughly-drawn black skull, and the white of the paper had been cleverly used to form its grinning teeth. Blake shrugged his shoulders, and thrust the threat in his pocket.

During his career he had received many such missives, some backed by all the deadly intent they spelled, some the mere outpourings of a weak and childish mentality. But in his heart he knew he had never received one which was meant more than was this.

And yet such was the man's determination that it never even occurred to him to relinquish the task he had undertaken, and which, after his interview with Alice Jefferson, must be a voluntary one.

He laid aside his hat and coat, and seated himself at the desk. Stuffing his pipe, he lighted it, and for many minutes sat puffing in silence, endeavouring to trace a way through the web of facts upon which he had stumbled.

Perhaps half an hour had passed by when a peal came at the street door-bell. Knowing Mrs. Bardell would have retired long since, Blake rose, and after slipping his revolver in the outside pocket of his lounge jacket, opened the door of the consulting-room, and strode along to the door.

As he drew back the bolt, he stepped back and gripped his revolver ready for use. He had no intention of being an easy mark for a further outrage by the gentlemen of the black skull; but on opening, the door, he saw that for once his caution had been unnecessary. On the step stood the lad Tim.

"Oh, it is you, Tim!" said Blake, "Come in, my lad. I hoped you would turn up."

"I came as soon as I could, Mr. Blake," answered the lad, as he followed Blake in. "I—"

"Wait, Tim, until we reach the consulting-room. Then let me have your report in full. Now, then," went on Blake, a few moments later when he had seated himself, "what is it?

"I know you were on duty at the rear of No. 12A, Fulton Terrace. I know you left there to make your way round to the front in order to report to Tinker. I know that you did not find him there, and I know that something caused you yourself to leave the terrace. You can begin there, and thus save time."

"All right, sir, I will. As you have said, I went round to report to Tinker as we had arranged I should. When I got there I could not see him, nor did he show up when I gave the signal we had fixed on. I knew that something had taken him away before he could tip me off.

"I was just figuring whether to remain on the watch in front, or return to the back, when I saw something which made me prick up my ears. It was a woman, who was standing on a corner opposite No. 12A.

"I thought at first she might be waiting for someone, but pretty soon I felt sure she was interested in the same house which I was watching. Then she moved and started to leave the terrace. I thought she was leaving it because I had appeared, though, of course, she could not see me then, sir, for I was concealed in an area-way. Anyway, I thought the best plan was for me to follow her for a bit. So I did, Mr. Blake."

"Ah! And what was the result, Tim?"

"I had a hard job to do it, sir. She led me a merry chase. Whether she fancied I might be behind or not, I don't know; but it wasn't long before I was sure that for some reason she was doubling and redoubling on her tracks. But I stuck to it, and after a while I saw her go into a house."

"That is good, my lad, good! Now then, where was the house?"

"It was at Queen Anne's Gate, sir. It is a big house. When she had gone through the main entrance, she turned and entered a door on the right. I waited there for about fifteen minutes, but she did not come out again.

"At the end of that time a motor drove up, and an old codger with a grey, pointed beard, and wearing evening clothes, got out. He went into the same place, and also opened the door on the right. I figured then I ought to come on here to report, Mr. Blake, so here I am,"

Almost before Tim had finished, Blake was on his feet.

"My lad," he said, "you have done more than well. It happens that you have struck something which I think will be of great value to me. It will require my immediate attention. If Tinker does as well on his mission, we should be a long way ahead in our investigation. I shall not ask you to do anything more to-night, Tim.

"There will be no further developments at Fulton Terrace for some hours at least. Go home to bed, my lad, and hold yourself in readiness. I may summon you at any moment. If you keep on this way I shall have to put you on the regular staff. Good-night!"

And Tim, utterly happy at the praise of the great detective, bade him good-night and departed. Not until the street door had closed after the lad did Blake make a move. Then he resumed his seat at the desk, and, drawing the desk 'phone towards him, gave a number.

A moment later he was listening to a clear, silvery voice at the other end of the wire.

"Hallo!" it said.

"Hallo!" answered Blake. "Is that Mademoiselle Yvonne speaking?"

"Yes; and you are Mr. Blake, are you not?"

"Yes, mademoiselle. I must ask your pardon for calling you up so late, but it concerns a matter of some importance. Is Graves at home?"

"Y-e-s. Did you wish to speak with him?"

And then Blake could not fathom why her tones were so hesitating.

"No, no," he answered quickly. "It is you I wished to see. I was wondering if I might ask you to strain a point, and receive me this evening. I know it is late, but I promise not to keep you long."

"Why, certainly, Mr. Blake. Uncle and I are here in the smoking-room by ourselves. Do come!"

"I shall be there inside of twenty minutes," responded Blake.

With that he hung up the receiver, and rose to his feet. He wasted little time in putting on his coat and hat, and once more adopting the precaution of taking his revolver, he hurried out. Not a taxi was in sight, but as Queen Anne's Gate was no great distance, and as he knew he could do it on foot in the quarter-hour, he set off at a brisk pace.

Arriving at his destination, he hurried in and pressed the button of the door on the right-hand side. Almost at once it was opened, and Blake saw Graves standing just within. He noticed at once that the older man looked strangely worn and haggard, and when he spoke Blake could detect a ring of forced lightness in his tones.

"Come in," he said, holding the door wide. "As usual, you almost beat the clock."

Blake laughed, and, entering, slipped off his coat.

"I certainly must apologise for calling at such an hour," he said, as he hung up his hat; "but, as a matter of fact, something has just been brought to my attention which made me wish to see Yvonne. I was afraid she might have retired."

"Oh, no! She has been writing. Come along. She is in the smoking-room."

Blake followed him down the hall to the room at the end. From the threshold he saw Yvonne sitting at the desk, but a quick glance told him it would be impossible to judge from her garments whether she had been out that evening or not.

She was dressed in a soft blue house-gown, and her feet were encased in tiny blue slippers. Certainly she had not been abroad in those garments. He did notice, however, that she was distinctly pale, and that the misty, blue eyes held shadows of worry —or was it fear? He could not tell.

She greeted him with all her usual warmth, and looking down deep into her eyes, he knew that if it were fear which they held it was no longer fear of him, so frankly and wistfully did they meet his. After apologising to her for his late call, Blake was about to speak further when Graves interrupted.

"If you will excuse me," he said, "I shall go along to the billiard-room, and knock the balls about for a bit. When you get through talking business, call me, and we will have a cigar before you go."

"Thanks," said Blake. "I shall be pleased."

As Graves took his departure, he turned back to Yvonne. She had not yet spoken a single word, and, during his conversation with Graves, had sat down at the desk. Blake drew up a chair facing her, and laying one hand on the polished mahogany of the desk again looked deep into her eyes.

Not until the distant click of the billiard-balls sounded did he speak. Then he leaned forward, and said in quiet tones:

"Yvonne, what is your interest in No. 12A. Fulton Terrace?"

For a single instant he thought she intended to flee, such a hunted look came into her eyes; but it passed at once, and she faced him bravely.

"I —I don't understand," she said waveringly.

"You do understand, Yvonne. Surely there are no conceivable circumstances where it is necessary for you to be evasive with me. Surely the past has proved that. Have we gone through so much together for nothing? Have we even faced death together for nothing? It is futile to even suggest that you don't trust me. I know you do. And I know, moreover, that you were at Fulton Terrace, watching No. 12A, for some time to-night. And, Yvonne —"

"Yes?" she whispered, gazing at him in fascinated dread.

"I can't prove it; but were you not only in Fulton Terrace, but in the study of No. 12A about midnight last night?"

"Oh! Oh! Oh!"

The short, sharp gasps came from Yvonne's innermost being as she listened to Blake's slow, torturing words. She looked at him, and looked away; she half-rose, but sank back; her face went even whiter than it had been.

Startled, Blake rose and unconsciously took her slim little hand in his.

"Forgive me, Yvonne," he said quietly. "I can see your nerves are strained. I should not have been so abrupt. But, Yvonne, I know now that my question struck the truth.

"Let me convince you that my attitude is only friendly. I am not seeking to pierce your secrets. You know I could never again be your enemy. But you also know what happened at No. 12A, Fulton Terrace last night, and that the police are using every resource known to ferret out the truth.

"I can assure you that so far no one but myself suspects that the individual who was surprised in the study was a woman, much less you. At the same time, one never knows what accident may cause them to stumble on the truth. Perhaps I know a great deal more of the whole affair than even you.

"I know absolutely that you had no hand in that terrible affair, yet you must know many things which would be of immense value to me. Come, Yvonne. Trust me as you have always trusted me.

"If you are shielding someone else, confide in me. You know I am safe, and together we can decide what is best to be done. Believe me, the police are sparing no efforts in this affair. It is the culmination of a series every one of which is so far unsolved. They are on their mettle now. Their prestige and their positions depend upon it.

"In this particular case I have a theory which I am certain has not occurred to them, nor do I think it will. But that theory I may prove with your assistance, and if there is anything vital to you, it can be dealt with before the police stumble upon it. Now will you confide in me?"

All the time Blake had been speaking Yvonne had been unconsciously tightening her hold upon his hand, as though in it she would find the strength and protection she sought. When he had finished his plea she looked up at him steadily. Her eyes never wavered as her other hand sought his, and she whispered:

"You know there is no being upon earth I trust as I trust you. Always you have been a true, chivalrous gentleman, and more than once a rock of refuge to me. It is unnecessary for me to tell you that.

"You know —you have known for a long time —what I feel for you. I say it again, nor do my eyes drop as I say it. I am not ashamed of it. Were my nature not what it is, I might have forgotten the past, but I am not one of those who forget. The flame burns as intensely to-day as it ever did. And nothing in this life will ever extinguish it.

"As to this other matter of which you speak. It is the truth. I was in Fulton Terrace to-night, and No. 12A was the object of my interest. I was also in the study there at midnight last night, when the police arrived. It is true that I am the second mysterious visitor to which the papers refer. How you discovered that it was not a man, and, further, that it was I, I do not profess even to guess. But it is the truth.

"And I will tell you more. My object in disguising myself as I did, and going secretly to No. 12A, was connected with Gilbert Jefferson."

"And I can tell you something else," put in Blake. "I can tell you, and I hope soon to prove, that the man found in the study at No. 12 A had been dead for some time when you got there,"

"That is true. I was terribly surprised and upset at the discovery, and had barely time to make my escape. But, Mr. Blake, don't ask me any more, I beseech you. There are reasons —reasons not strictly connected with me, but personal reasons, all the same —which make it impossible for me to tell you any more about my visit. I will add this, however.

"My interest in Gilbert Jefferson's study arose through business matters. I have had an interest in the Jefferson Silk Company for about two years. A few months ago I began to fear he was jeopardising the future of the company by gambling in shares. That led me to place one of my agents in his office as a clerk, in order to get a true idea of the present standing of the company and the condition of its finances.

"It was because of the surprise occasioned by that agent's report that I was impelled to make a secret visit to Gilbert Jefferson's house. But before I went, although I know it was risky, I assure you I had not the faintest notion I should stumble upon Gilbert Jefferson's dead body."

For some moments Blake sat in silence, pondering over what she had said. It came as no little surprise to him to discover that she was the woman who held such a large number of shares in the silk company.

She must therefore be the one with whom Hammerton Palmer was beginning a struggle for the control of the company. That placed them both in the same camp, and upon a mutual plane of offence and defence against Hammerton Palmer, the man who now loomed more than ever in Blake's eyes as the central figure in the whole drama.

It seemed to him more vital than ever that he and Yvonne should join forces, and, after an unreserved discussion of the facts in the possession of each, form their plans. He could not imagine what personal reason held her back, but calculated that if he took the initiative, she might yield.

At any rate, he held one tremendous card in his hand, and instead of holding it until the last, decided to play it first. If that failed to move her, then he must adopt other means. And it seemed to pass unheeded by both that Yvonne's hands still lay passive in Blake's.

Having decided on his next move, Blake again looked up,

"Yvonne," he said slowly, "I am going to say something to you which I feel safe in saying is undreamed of by the police. It may be suspected by one other individual. That I do not know as yet, but I do know it is unnecessary to ask you to lock it in your heart and keep it there. It is this:

"Would, it make any difference in your attitude if I said that, in my opinion, the man whom you saw in the study at No. 12A was not Gilbert Jefferson at all, and that Gilbert Jefferson is not dead, but living!"

At that moment a great gasp came from behind Blake, and he swung sharply as tense tones which he hardly recognised as those of Graves rang out.

"Then in Heaven's name who was the man who was murdered?" he cried, and Blake had barely time to spring towards him and catch him before Graves crumpled up in a heap on the floor.

## The Tenth Chapter.   Yvonne's Story —The Death Club —Tinker's Report.

THERE was no need for Blake to sign to Yvonne to assist him. Almost as soon as he had sprung forward to catch Graves, she had hastened to the sideboard, and had poured out a stiff dose of brandy. She handed it to Blake, who was supporting Graves' head, and in silence he poured it between the unconscious man's lips.

The strong spirit coursed down his throat, and he stirred. His lids flickered for a moment as though about to open; then they remained shut, and, instead, the two watchers were startled to hear his voice come clear and strong.

"The Death Club! The Death Club! Hammerton Palmer," he said.

And brief as the words were, there was a sinister something in their suggestion which made even Blake recoil at the thought.

Almost immediately he had again forced some more brandy between Graves' teeth, for he had no desire to acquire information through unguarded lips. Yet now he began to see dimly why it was Yvonne had fought so hard to guard the secret which was hers —and Graves'.

Again the closed lids wavered, and this time opened.

"I am sorry," muttered Graves, trying to sit up as he recognised Blake. "I thought you and Yvonne had probably finished your conversation. Came along to see. Must have fainted. Haven't been too well lately. Sorry! Deucedly silly of me."

And neither Blake nor Yvonne made any mention of the startling words he had uttered as he fell unconscious. Both of them tacitly avoided the subject, and when Blake suggested that Graves should retire, Yvonne backed him up.

Graves seemed only too glad to do so, and when Yvonne had accompanied him to the foot of the stairs, she returned to find Blake sitting in a low chair, his brows wrinkled in thought. Closing the door, she locked it, and stood with her back to it.

As she leant against it, regarding him with her great misty eyes, which at night looked like shadowy woodland pools of violet, her attitude was so utterly weary and appealing, that a great wave of desire to take her in his arms and comfort her rushed over Blake, and it needed all the iron control the man possessed to keep himself in check.

Perhaps Yvonne realised the inward struggle Blake was undergoing; perhaps something of what he felt showed in those usually carefully-masked features; perhaps this made her pride rise up and disdain to precipitate that which her whole being longed for and her heart ached for. At any rate, she left the door and stumbled wearily across to the desk. Seating herself, she faced him.

"It is useless to attempt to gloss over what has just happened," she said dully. "If you are prepared to listen now, I will tell you all I know about this affair. But before I do so, will you please tell me if you were quite certain of your ground when you stated your conviction that Gilbert Jefferson, was still alive?"

Blake bent his head.

"I stated it then, and I state it now, Yvonne. In my opinion, Gilbert Jefferson is not only alive, but in the City."

"If that is so, it makes a tremendous difference to me," she said, with more life in her tones. "It does away at one stroke with much of the doubt and suspense which has racked me all day.

"But since uncle's collapse here on hearing that, it is useless to keep what I know from you any longer. It spoke for itself, though, truly, I know little. But what I do know I will tell you, and, if I can, will help you. And I shall keep back nothing."

Slowly, but without pause, Yvonne began, and related all that had happened from the time Channing had come with his report the previous evening until Blake's arrival. She told of the financial condition of the silk company, both at the present time and seven months before. She dwelt on what Blake already knew from Formby Mott about Gilbert Jefferson's gambling in shares, and his suddenly changed financial position during the past seven months.

"It was only when uncle showed he knew much, and refused to tell me what that was, that I made up my mind to find out the truth at any cost," she went on. "I was afraid for him, and I was afraid for myself. That was why I went to Fulton Terrace to-night.

"As you probably know, I learned nothing there. But when I got home I found more in five minutes than I had hoped to find in as many days. It was a letter which had come addressed to uncle. In itself it was ordinary enough; but something —I don't know what — impelled me to examine it closely.

"It was then that I noticed it had been readdressed to uncle from Maida Vale, where we have not lived for a long time. That recalled several similar instances to my mind, and I sat down to think.

"It was not long before I began to remember that about half a dozen letters had come in the same way during as many months. A further searching of my memory, and the remembrance of several unimportant happenings, enabled me to place these arrivals more definitely, and that was just previous to the end of each month.

"Now, if uncle were expecting regular monthly communications from a source with which he wished to keep in touch, I calculated he would naturally give them his present address. Since these missives all continued to go to our old address, I concluded he did not wish the writer to know where he lived at present.

"I don't know why I connected the arrival of the last one with the date of the murder at No. 12A, Fulton Terrace, but I did; and, following that, something —I don't know what —impelled me to open the one which came to-night. I did so, and when I read the contents, I thought I began to see light. Before proceeding further I will show you what it was."

As she spoke, Yvonne opened a drawer of the desk and drew out an envelope. She handed it across to Blake, and a thrill ran through him as he saw that the typewritten address on the envelope was not only pale blue in colour, but that several letters showed the same faults as those on the envelopes received, that same night by Alice Jefferson. Truly the scent was growing warm.

Swiftly he drew out the enclosed sheet of folded paper. It was perfectly plain, and, like the envelope, typewritten.

This is what met his gaze:

"An extraordinary meeting of the D.C. will be held at the usual place to-morrow evening at ten o'clock. All members are specially requested to attend. A division of profits will be made, after which urgent business will be discussed."

And for a signature there was a tiny skull drawn in black ink— an exact reproduction of the one which had been sketched at the end of the threat which had been left at Baker Street that evening.

When he had finished reading it, Blake laid it back on the desk, remarking, as he did so:

"It was fortunate, indeed, that you opened it, Yvonne. It happens that it coincides most strikingly with some facts I have gathered, but those I will discuss with you later. Proceed with your story, please."

"I think that is about all there is to tell you," she said.

"What D.C. meant I had no idea, but something told me it had to do with Gilbert Jefferson. I was actually pondering over this very thing, and trying to make up my mind to confront uncle with it, when you rang up.

"Of course, what he said when he lay unconscious has told me a lot. Undoubtedly, D.C. means Death Club, and I can only surmise that Hammerton Palmer has some connection with it, as has my uncle. What it is, what it means, or what its purpose may be, I have no idea; but whatever it is, I am certain my uncle's connection with it is of a most unwilling nature. That is all."

"And it is a great deal, Yvonne, thank you for your confidence. Several points have been made clearer by what you have told me, and, if all goes as I hope, it won't be long before I get sufficient proof to put my hands on the man I now know to be the prime factor in this, and, I think, in many another affair.

"I do not intend going into the whole history of it to-night. I shall tell you what facts are necessary as I proceed with my plans, but later I promise to tell you all. Now let us deal with this letter.

"Firstly, I can tell you for a certainty that this letter and envelope were typed on a machine belonging to Hammerton Palmer.

"Secondly, I feel confident he is the head and tail of the organisation, the existence of which I have suspected for some time.

"Until now it has been absolutely impossible to get material upon which to act. They have covered up their tracks too thoroughly. Their organisation must be well-nigh perfect and their discipline of the most rigid description.

"But now we have something definite to go upon. We have here proof that Graves is a member, though apparently he fulfils his membership through fear of the consequences. If the murder at 12A, Fulton Terrace is a sample of the methods of the Death Club, I must say I can hardly blame him for his feeling.

"We know, further, that an extraordinary meeting is called for to-morrow night at the usual place. Now in your relation of what you had discovered, you told me that when Graves spoke of Gilbert Jefferson he said, he knew he was to meet his death, yet he did not know Jefferson personally.

"That caused me to think, and, applying my knowledge of the ritual of secret organisations, I have thought it is just probable the reason for that may be because when members attend a meeting of the

Death Club they are masked. If that is so, it suggests a risky but attractive plan to me."

"What is that?"

"That, disguised as Graves, I attend the meeting of the Death Club to-morrow night."

"No —no, Mr. Blake. If you were found out your life would not be worth a moment's purchase."

"They have already sentenced me to death, Yvonne," said Blake quietly. "Only to-night they almost succeeded in accomplishing their purpose." Briefly he then told her of what had happened while he was on his way to Fulton Terrace. "So you see," he continued, with a smile, "the fight must now be carried into the territory of the enemy. Don't you agree with me?"

"It is so terribly risky," she objected. Then suddenly her attitude changed. "But perhaps it is the best plan. How will you manage it?"

"That is where you come in. You must go to Graves. Tell him we know all. Make him confess where the meeting is to be held, and what formalities are necessary before entering. Discover if there is a password. Then leave the rest to me."

"All right, I will do so. I think I can get from him the information you want. Doubtless, his tongue has been tied by ridiculous oaths as well as fear, but I shall get the information we need in some way."

"That will be a big step forward, Yvonne; I shall make my arrangements accordingly, and, if you will name an hour to-morrow afternoon, I will come round in order to talk over the final arrangements. Perhaps by this time to-morrow night we shall be able to put our hands on Hammerton Palmer."

"Then to find Gilbert Jefferson if he still lives, and to discover who the man was who was murdered at No. 12A, Fulton Terrace, and who it was who did the deed. Though, as to the latter, I have a very strong suspicion."

"Will three o'clock in the afternoon suit you?"

"Perfectly."

"Then if you will come at that hour I shall try to have the information you need."

"Very well. And now I will go."

Yvonne rose to accompany him to the door. When she had helped him into his coat Blake turned, and took both her hands in his.

"Good-night, little girl," he said softly. "Keep up your courage."

And with that he was gone.

For one long moment after the door closed Yvonne stood poised as though she must call him back, then her arms dropped wearily to her sides, and she turned back towards the smoking-room. But, as she made her way down the hall, she might have been heard to murmur:

"I will get the information he needs, and, if he wishes, he may attend the meeting of the Death Club disguised as uncle. But there are other members of that club, and unless I am greatly mistaken, there will be another genuine member absent besides uncle. For, by hook or by crook, I go to that perilous meeting to-morrow night with the man I love."

.       .       .       .       .

When Blake arrived at Baker Street he was surprised to see a light in the consulting-room. The first thought was that Tinker must have returned and was waiting up; the second thought was that it might be a ruse of those who had condemned him to death.

On entering the room he found his first thought to be the right one. There sat Tinker on the floor, a large basin of hot water on one side of him and Pedro on the other.

But such an object as he was would be hard to find off the battlefield. A soiled blood-stained bandage was bound about his head, his face was begrimed with dirt and blood; one arm was in a sling, and his clothes were in tatters.

He was in the act of bathing his injured hand when Blake entered, and, though he tried to grin cheerfully, the attempt twisted his face into a strange and awful caricature of his usual expression.

"Well, for Heaven's sake!" began Blake, on first catching sight of him. Then, seeing the bloodstains, he hurried forward, "Why, my lad, what has happened to you? Are you severely injured?"

"A little knocked about, guv'nor," answered Tinker, with another terrible grin, "but still in the ring. I had a close shave but got clear, and I've got a report to make that ought to interest you."

"Out with it, my lad, while I bathe your wounds," said Blake, taking off his coat and kneeling down. "Now, then, what is it?"

"Well, to begin with, guv'nor, I can tell you where to put your hands on a man who seems to have a lot of personal property belonging to the late Gilbert Jefferson."

"Do you speak of the man you followed from Fulton Terrace this evening?" asked Blake quickly.

"Yes, guv'nor. How did you know?"

"Never mind now how I knew. Begin at the beginning and tell me all that has occurred."

"All right, sir."

Tinker began with his arrival in Fulton Terrace, and told Blake all that had happened from that up to the moment when had looked up from the iron chest in the loft-room over the old warehouse by the London Docks, to find himself gazing into the barrel of an automatic.

"I can tell you, guv'nor, I thought the game was up. If I ever saw murder in a man's eyes I saw it in his, and it didn't take him long to show me what his intention was. Without a word, or the slightest warning, he stepped forward, then fired point-blank at me. That is how I got this." And Tinker touched his temple.

"It gouged out a bit, but luckily it glanced off. For a moment I was stunned by the shock of the bullet, but when I saw him getting ready to fire again I pulled myself together. I was nearly blinded with the blood. I drew my own revolver and opened fire. I missed the first shot, and then he suddenly extinguished the light he was carrying.

"After that there began a duel in the dark such as I never want to experience again. I knew he would think I would at once take advantage of the darkness to creep away and try to make my way to the door. Instead of doing that I stayed exactly where I was.

"It seemed like an hour before I heard a move from him. It was pitch black, and that didn't make the situation any more cheerful, I can tell you. After a while I heard a move over near the door, and I knew his patience had given out first. Now that I had him located I decided to make the first move.

"I had extinguished my pocket-torch, but had it near; I reached for it as quietly as I could, and got my finger on the switch. Then, holding my revolver ready, I pressed the switch, and the light hit him the first time. He was still standing at the door, and no sooner had the light found him than he began to open fire again.

"I fired back, and for about ten seconds we had a pretty hot revolver duel. I got him once in the leg I know, and, although none of his bullets struck me, I could hear them plumping against the iron lid of the box behind me.

"Then one of his bullets caught the torch fair on the lens. It put it out instantly, and not only that, but the shock numbed my left arm and made it useless, as you can see. It aches badly still, but I guess it is

129

nothing serious.

"After that the duel kept up in the dark for some time, then I stopped firing, because all my ammunition was gone. I think he must have figured this to be the case, for he lighted his candle and closed the door. By this time I could hardly see on account of the blood in my eyes, and my head swam terribly from loss of blood and the pain in my arm. At any rate, he came across towards me.

"When he got close he raised his revolver as though to strike me down with the butt-end. Then he did strike, I dodged, and in a moment we were into a rough and tumble. He was a strong man, and, even if I hadn't been wounded, I should have had my hands full to wriggle away from him.

"As it was, I saw after a minute that he was getting the better of me. I made one last effort to get away, but he bent my head back and struck me repeatedly in the face. That finished me, and the last thing I remembered for some time was his still pounding me.

"When I came to I found myself lying on a heap of blankets in a loft-room not unlike the one in which the fight had taken place. It wasn't the same, though.

"In the first place, it wasn't so clean; and, in the second place, it had no iron chest. I figured out that it must be the loft-room he had entered when I saw him on the roof. I found out afterwards that I was right.

"It only took me a few seconds to discover that my hands were bound. The man with was in the room, and was busy at an old fireplace in the corner. When he saw I was conscious he spoke.

" 'It was a lucky thing I had to return to the other room for matches, you young thief," he said, "Otherwise I suppose you would have filled your pockets with gold and decamped. As it is, you will never steal again.'

"His words showed me he had no idea of my identity and that I had followed him from Fulton Terrace. He thought I was just a neighbourhood lad who had turned thief, so I let him think so.

"He was busy burning papers in the fireplace, and, for a while he did not speak again. After he had finished burning the papers he took some clothes down off a peg on the wall and began to burn those, too. It wasn't hard to see that he was making a thorough clean up of someone's belongings. Whether they were his own or not I don't know, guv'nor. After a while he spoke again.

" 'I will tell you now what I am going to do with you,' he said. 'It happens that I am leaving England for good to-morrow night. This room and the room where I caught you are mine. They will not be entered, perhaps, for months.

" 'I am not going to kill you, but for certain reasons I am not going to permit you to get away. What I am going to do is this: I am going to leave your hands bound and lock you in here. You may live two days, you may live a week, but eventually you will die.

" 'Nor am I going to leave you either food or water. I shall be busy all day to-morrow, but before I leave here at midnight to-morrow I shall come again to see you. After I leave, if you can escape, you are welcome to your freedom.

" 'That is all, my thieving young friend. If you do get free after I leave visit the other room, you are welcome to all you will find. Now good-night, and pleasant dreams.'

"With that he left, guv'nor, and locked the door behind him. I knew I was in a tight hole then all right, for while he had been talking I had made a discovery. The man was mad.

"There was madness in his manner, and madness in his eyes. If he had been sane I shouldn't have felt half so nervous, but to be the prisoner of a madman like that —well, guv'nor, I don't want to experience it again I can tell you.

"As soon as he was gone I began to figure on escaping. I knew I must do so before to-morrow night, for without food or water I should be a lot weaker and, besides, there was no telling what new plans might occur to the madman. I thought over every method I had ever heard of, but there was nothing at hand with which to put them into practice.

"Then after a bit my eyes fell on the remains of the fire, and an idea came to me. I rolled off the blankets and, by turning over and over, finally managed to get close to the fireplace. With my toes I drew out several live coals, caused by bits of boxes he had been burning, and letting these lie in a heap on the hearth, I twisted myself round until I got my wrists near them. Then I set my teeth and pressed down hard against them.

"It almost made me go unconscious again, guv'nor, but I stuck to it and just when I thought I must give up, I felt my bonds part, and I was free. My wrists were burned badly, as you can see, but I guess that was a small price to pay for escape from the hands of that madman.

"After that, the door was comparatively easy. He had taken the key with him and that left the lock free. I had my 'spider' instrument in my pocket, and it didn't take long to force the bolt back, although it took longer than usual, because I had to stop from time to time, my wrists hurt so.

"When I got the door open, I slipped out and closed it after me. Lighting a match I saw that I was in a small passage similar to the one leading from the other loft-room. At the far end was a flight of stairs leading to the attic above.

"I went up these and found myself in an attic exactly like the other. There was a skylight overhead, and hanging from it, was a rope ladder, proving that the madman certainly intended coming back before he left England —if he told the truth when he said that. I climbed up and managed to get on to the roof.

"Then I crawled along until I reached the wires which crossed it. So far I had seen no signs of the madman, and, once I got well started along the wires, I didn't care much.

"Well, sir, I scrambled on to them and started for the pole. I made the journey without a hitch, and climbed down the cross trees until I reached the bottom one. When I got to it I wound my legs round the pole and began to slide down.

"As I came opposite the window of the loft-room, where I had first seen the madman, I caught a fleeting glimpse of him doing something at the table. And, guv'nor, what do you think that was?"

"What was it, my lad?"

"He was piling the sovereigns I had seen into canvas bags. That was all I saw; then I hit the pavement with a bump and made tracks for Baker Street. That is the story, guv'nor."

"I needn't tell you, my lad, that you have indeed done well, You have had a very narrow escape from a fate I don't care to contemplate, for I know a little more of this affair than you, and I can assure you that the man you refer to as the madman meant every word he said. Moreover, I am quite convinced he spoke the truth when he said he was leaving England for good to-morrow night."

"But guv'nor, who is he? What is he? And what connection has he with the murder at Fulton Terrace? Is he the man who murdered Gilbert Jefferson?"

"You yourself have described what he is, my lad. He is a

madman —mad through his own folly and the machinations of a fiend in human form. As to who he is I will tell you.

"You were quite right in concluding he was no wharf labourer, but instead was a masquerader. So he is, for, my lad, if my theories and deductions are right, that man is none other than Gilbert Jefferson himself."

HOW Yvonne was to gain the information she desired from Graves Blake had no idea, but he went ahead on his plans to attend the meeting of the Death Club on the following evening as assuredly as though he already had her report in hand.

It was sufficient for him to know that she had promised to find out what he needed. As did she, he imagined if Graves really had a connection with that mysterious organisation, he would doubtless consider his lips sealed by oaths of secrecy, and the undoubted fear which filled him would go a long way towards keeping them sealed. But he trusted to Yvonne's ingenuity to overcome that obstacle, and, in his heart, he knew she would use every resource of her art.

When he had finished doctoring Tinker, and had stemmed the lad's flow of excited questions about Gilbert Jefferson by the curt command to wait and he would hear all, he saw the lad to bed, and then retired himself.

He was astir early the next morning, for he had a busy day ahead of him. His first move was to make another visit to Inspector Thomas at Scotland Yard. There he spent a busy two hours going over every scrap of evidence which the police had gathered regarding the series of murders and disappearances which had occurred during the past several months.

Not only that, but he made an exhaustive search into the records of all unsolved murders for the preceding three years, and, when he had finished, he had a mass of notes and dates in his notebook which would have puzzled any but himself to decipher.

Leaving the Yard, he went on to the City, where he made a call at the offices of a large mercantile agency. There he asked for, and received, a detailed report of Hammerton Palmer, the financier, extending over five years. That done he went on to Somerset House, and from there drove to the offices of Formby Mott, the lawyer.

At the latter place he inspected a copy of Gilbert Jefferson's will, and carefully perused both of the latter's insurance policies. When he had finished he turned to the lawyer:

"I wonder if you will do something for me, Mr. Mott, and not ask the reason? I am prepared to assure you that it is entirely in the interests of your client, Miss Jefferson, and that in any event it works in with your own plans."

134

"What is that, Mr. Blake?"

"It is this. Will you telephone to Hammerton Palmer? Ask him if he will come to your office, and bring with him the document which he claims to hold from Gilbert Jefferson, in which the latter charges his niece to be guided by Palmer in her dealings with the Jefferson Silk Company."

"Do you wish to be here when he comes?" asked Mott, with wrinkled brows.

"No. And, moreover, I don't want him to know I have been here. Will you do that?"

"You are sure it holds nothing detrimental to the interests of my client, Miss Jefferson?"

"On the contrary, I am prepared to pledge you my word that it is in her interests."

"Then I don't mind doing as you ask. In fact, I wish to have a look at that document anyway. If Palmer is to advise her in her affairs I, as her solicitor and one of the executors of the will, may clash with him. One moment, and I will call him on the 'phone, and let you know what he says."

As he spoke the lawyer drew the desk 'phone towards him and gave a number. In a few minutes Blake heard him say:

"Is that the office of Mr. Hammerton Palmer?"

Evidently the reply was in the affirmative, for he next said:

"Connect me with Mr. Palmer. What? This is Mr. Formby Mott speaking.

There was a few moments' wait, then the lawyer said:

"Is that Mr. Palmer speaking? This is Formby Mott." "Yes." "Can you make it convenient to drop around to my office, Mr. Palmer, and bring with you the document you hold from Gilbert Jefferson, of which you spoke at the offices of the Silk Company yesterday? You can? Thank you. About how soon do you expect to be here?" "Within half an hour." "All right. I shall be on the look out for you. Good-bye."

With that he hung up the receiver and turned to Blake.

"You heard, of course?"

Blake nodded and rose.

"Yes. Since he will be here within half an hour, it means that he will start at once. Therefore I shall be going."

"Will you return later?"

"Perhaps. I can't say yet. In any event, you will hear from me within a day or two, Mr. Mott. Thanks very much for obliging me. I shall be pleased to return the compliment at any time."

"Oh, don't mention it." answered Mott rising and shaking hands. "It was sufficient for me to know that it was in the interests of my client."

When Blake left the lawyer's offices, he hailed a taxi, and, instead of telling the chauffeur to drive to Baker Street, he ordered him to go to the office of Hammerton Palmer. Outside the entrance to the big building the taxi drew up and Blake descended.

"Wait here," he said briefly.

Entering, he sought the lift, and was shot up to the sixth floor. There he emerged and walked along the tiled passage until, ahead of him, he saw on a door the sign: "Hammerton Palmer, Financier."

As he drew nearer, he saw several other doors along the passage bearing the same sign, but with the exception of the first one all bore the additional word "Private."

Turning the handle of the first one, Blake opened the door. Inside he saw what was obviously an outer public office. Behind a wire cage were a couple of clerks footing up ledgers, while over in one corner was a girl pounding away at a typewriter.

With one swift glance Blake took in the make of the machine, then he strode briskly to the cage.

"Good-morning." he said. "I have come to inspect your typewriters. I see you are still using the National."

"Oh, yes!" answered one of the clerks. "You will find one or two of them pretty badly out of alignment, I guess. Miss Smith, this gentleman wishes to inspect your typewriter," he called to the girl in the corner.

She rose at once and Blake, walking across, sat down before the machine. Slipping in a sheet of paper he began writing a series of meaningless sentences upon it, bringing in every character on the keyboard.

The clerks had returned to their work, and the typist stood watching him apathetically, none of them dreaming for a moment, that the man who pounded so energetically upon the machine was other than a representative of the firm who had made it.

Yet not once had Blake made the statement that he was. All he had said was that he had come to inspect the typewriters. They, of their own accord, had jumped to the conclusion that he must come from the firm which had supplied them, otherwise, he would not be there.

Blake had no idea of the make of the machines used in Palmer's offices when he first entered. His glance at the one in the corner had told him that, and he had taken a pure gambling chance on the others being of the same make. Even if they weren't, he counted on his own ingenuity to enable him to get a sample of the work of each.

When he had finished his inspection of the machine in the outer office, he thrust the sample of the work he had done in his pocket, and jotted down a few notes regarding its condition.

"A mechanic will come and attend to it," he said, turning to the typist; then he again approached the desk. "Will it be convenient for me to inspect the others now?" he asked the clerk to whom he had spoken before.

"Certainly. Come this way, please."

Blake went round the wire cage and followed the clerk through a door. Inside was another office where several clerks were at work. In this room there were two machine's, one a National, and the other of a make which had but recently come on the market. After his inspection of the National, Blake turned to his guide.

"Do you mind if I take a sample of the work of that other machine? It is a rival of the National, and I haven't seen what it can do yet."

"Go ahead if you wish."

Quickly Blake rattled off a page of writing. Then he rose. They passed through a large office, which was evidently the inner general office. It contained four machines, and for a quarter of an hour Blake was busy rattling off samples of work from each, and ostentatiously jotting down notes regarding their condition.

He began to see that his inspection would have to be hastened if it were to finish before the return of Hammerton Palmer from the offices of Formby Mott, the lawyer. The next office was the cashier's, and Blake breathed easier when he saw it contained no machine.

As yet he had not seen anything in the samples of work he had taken which had quickened his interest; but, although there was now only one room left to inspect —Hammerton Palmer's private office —he had by no means given up hope.

After knocking on the door, the clerk turned the handle and

entered. The room itself was most sumptuously furnished, proving that its occupant knew to perfection the art of outward impressions.

At present it was vacant.

"Mr. Palmer's own typist is out to lunch," said the clerk; "but I guess you can go ahead and inspect the machine if you wish. At the same time, I wish you would be as rapid as possible. Mr. Palmer may return at any moment, and he might not care foe examination of the machine being made in the absence of the operator."

"I shall not be five minutes," answered Blake.

Swiftly he strode across the office and lifted the cover off the machine. Then he slipped in a sheet of paper, and rapidly ran his fingers over the keys, taking an imprint from each character.

And as he did so his pulses quickened, for the colour of the type was pale blue, and in several of the letters which he had written were the same peculiarities he had seen on the envelopes received by Alice Jefferson, as well as the one sent to Graves and opened by Yvonne.

Before taking out the sheet of paper, he wrote what would have looked from even close at hand nothing but a meaningless array of letters; but, when separated properly, they spelled much that was important to Blake,

This was the array:

"MissAliceJeffersonNo12AFultonTerraceSW."

In places he used capitals where they should have been used, and in places he didn't. The lack of word spacing made it look like one long confused array; but in one of the letters it contained Blake saw something which told him more than anything else. One leg of the capital A was broken off.

Finishing this, Blake drew out the sheet of paper, and thrust it in his pocket with the others. Then he picked up his hat.

"Thank you," he said, turning to the clerk. "I have finished now."

"All right. You can go out at this door if you wish."

The clerk opened the door leading from the passage into the corridor, and Blake passed out. A moment later he was hurrying towards the lift, murmuring as he went:

"I have one bit of proof, anyway, Hammerton Palmer. I can prove now that the typewriting machine in your private office was used to write the letter to Alice Jefferson, in which you enclosed Gilbert Jefferson's command to her not to make investigations in the event of his death.

"I can also prove that the notice of the meeting of the Death Club sent to Graves was written on the same machine. Now I wonder just what means you used to get those self-protective documents out of Gilbert Jefferson.

"Both the one commanding his niece to be guided by you in her business affairs, and the one charging her not to investigate the circumstances of his death, show distinct forethought on the part of someone, and I think that someone is you.

"Why you should desire to control her shares in the silk company is obvious; but why it should be so much to your interest to suppress all investigations regarding the murder at Fulton Terrace is only beginning to be clear to me. Perhaps to-night, when I have reached the inner circle of your Death Club, I shall know more."

It was close on two o'clock when Blake reached Baker Street. He went first to see Tinker, who was still in bed, but who was now preparing to get up. Then he had a hurried lunch, and, after running through what letters had arrived in his absence, 'phoned for his car to take him to Queen Anne's Gate.

It was just on three when he reached there, Yvonne herself opened the door to him, and together they moved along the hall to the smoking-room at the far end.

No sooner had they entered than Yvonne closed and locked the door behind her. Then she turned to him.

"I have all the information you need," she said, in low tones. "The meeting of the Death Club takes place at the residence of Hammerton Palmer at ten o'clock this evening. I have persuaded uncle to remain away, and to permit you to go in his place.

"I have also procured the names of a few of the members. You were right about his being a member through dread of the consequences if he refused to attend. Hammerton Palmer is the head and front of the organisation, and, from what I can gather, rules with a rod of iron. You will be astonished at some of the names of the members who belong.

"This is all I have secured so far; but if success attends you to-night, and this organisation is broken up, I have no doubt we can get the whole history of the club from uncle. He is still in bed, and has some fever, so I did not press him too hard to-day. Here is the list of names."

Blake took the slip of paper which she handed to him, and read the half-dozen names written upon it. He whistled in surprise as he read them, for some of them were the names of people very high up indeed in the social and political life of the City.

He handed it back to her; but she motioned him to keep it; so, thrusting it in his pocket, he said:

"I needn't tell you what your information means to me, Yvonne. I shall certainly attend the meeting of the Death Club to-night. I myself have secured a good deal of information to-day, and I think that before we have finished we shall have Mr. Hammerton Palmer in a corner from which all his money or all his influence will fail to extricate him.

"With the facts you have already gained, and those you expect to gain, together with the case I am preparing, I will wager the final result will be the unfolding of as gigantic a criminal conspiracy as was ever conceived in the City of London.

"And now I must get away to prepare for to-night. Rest assured I shall come to you as soon as the meeting of the Death Club is over, providing, of course, that no accidents occur."

And as he departed Blake saw the odd little smile which hovered on Yvonne's lips.

Lying on the floor by the table was a body. (Chapter 12.)

IT was ten o'clock the same evening. At the sumptuous residence of Hammerton Palmer in Park Lane dinner had been served earlier than usual, and most of the servants had been given a night out.

Only the old and trusted butler was on duty above stairs. As soon as the dining-room had been cleared he had busied himself arranging the great room as though he anticipated a further influx of guests.

The big table had been covered by a huge pad of green baize[1]. The massive light fixture overhead had been draped with thin silk of the same colour, causing the room to be shrouded in a dim green light.

Around the table he had drawn up several chairs —nine in all. At the head of the table was one chair alone, and, reposing on the green baize cloth in front of it, a small box. That was all.

When these arrangements had been completed the butler took up his place in the hall. The great grandfather clock in a niche of the staircase boomed out the hour of ten before he moved. Then he stirred, and, almost at the same instant, a subdued buzz came from a bell down the hall.

The butler moved softly along to the front door and opened it. Two gentlemen in evening-dress were at once admitted, and followed the butler to a room opening off the hall.

Scarcely had they disappeared when the bell buzzed again. This time a single gentleman was admitted, and he too was shown into a room off the hall.

Just then the door of the other room opened, and the two who had first arrived came out. They were garbed in evening-dress; but their features were hidden by black masks, which stretched from forehead to chin. They passed down the hall and entered the dining-room, where they seated themselves in silence.

From that on there were several more arrivals in the space of a few minutes. As each entered he was shown into a separate room by the butler, from which he emerged a few moments later wearing a mask, to take up his place in the silent gathering in the dining-room.

---

[1] a type of thick cloth made of wool that is usually green, used especially for covering card tables and billiard, snooker or pool tables.

When eight in all had arrived the butler pressed a button set in the wall, and almost at once a door at the far end opened. A man garbed as were the others, and also wearing a mask, appeared, and made his way towards the dining-room.

Before entering he beckoned to the butler, and whispered:

"How many?"

"Eight, sir —the full number."

"Very well. See that we are not disturbed."

With that he opened the door, and made his way in silence to the vacant seat at the head of the table. Guarding the same silence, he sat down and drew the silver box before him; then, through the holes in the mask, his eyes wandered down one side of the table and up the other, regarding slowly and fixedly each masked countenance.

For a few moments his fingers toyed with the silver box; but finally he lifted his head and, as his voice issued from beneath his mask, there was one, at least, at that table who recognised the tones as those of Hammerton Palmer.

"Gentlemen," he said slowly and distinctly, "there will be many of you —perhaps all —who will wonder why an urgent and extraordinary meeting of this club has been called tonight. In a few minutes you will understand the reason, for, before going ahead with other matters, it is my purpose to explain.

"Counting myself, there are nine of us here to-night. At our last meeting there were ten. Since then you have read in the papers that one of our members has passed from us, I speak of Number Six, and I think you all know whom I mean.

"As I said, you have all read of his passing, and, no doubt your minds harked back to the last meeting, when Number Six was the member who drew the black skull. You know what that meant. You expected to read of his death; but, gentlemen, this meeting has been called to-night for several reasons, one of the principal being to inform you that what you have read in the papers is untrue. Number Six is not dead, but living.

"He drew the black skull. He knew what he must do, but he did not do it. He flinched from it. Instead, he conceived a plot which he thought to be perfect. The man of whose death you have read is an unknown individual.

"Number Six made him the victim. This I suspected, and, by accident, discovered to be true. I shall tell you how, then you must decide what steps we are to take.

"When I read of the death of Number Six I, as no doubt each of you, was surprised to read that it was murder. As far as this organisation knew he had not flinched from doing his duty, and that step was unnecessary.

"I called at his house as soon as possible; and there discovered that, in accordance with the rules of the club, his affairs had been arranged in order that on his death the club should benefit by at least half. This half was, as I have said, intact.

"But I discovered another thing, gentlemen. I discovered that only a day or two before his death Number Six had drawn twenty thousand pounds from the bank. This in itself aroused my suspicions; but when I discovered further that every penny of that had been drawn in gold, my suspicions deepened into Certainty.

"Knowing as I did that we should have read of suicide, not murder, I had already made up my mind that there was something queer. Needless to say, I lost no time in endeavouring to discover more. I found out that, in addition to the police having the case in hand, the private investigator, Sexton Blake, also was following it up.

"I went to see him, but discovered nothing from him. At the same time I became convinced that something had caused him to suspect the truth, so I acted without consulting the club. Before I left I placed on his desk a black skull. You know what that meant.

"That same evening there was a terrific explosion in Baker Street. Someone had hurled a bomb from a passing motor, and Sexton Blake escaped death by inches. At the same time, the message of the skull has not been withdrawn.

"I also took measures to have him withdrawn from the case. You all know of the document exacted from each member on joining the club. This document I sent at once to the niece of Number Six. All this time I was endeavouring to fathom the mystery of Number Six, and, as I said, pure chance to-day gave me the explanation.

"I was in the East End of the City in a steamship office. While I was waiting, gentlemen, I saw a man enter and approach the counter. He was dressed as a wharf labourer, and at first did not receive a second glance from me. He inquired the price of a passage to West Africa, and as he spoke something in his tones attracted my attention.

"I surveyed him more closely then, and, gentlemen, in that wharf labourer, shaven and disguised though he was, I recognised our late member, Number Six. Now you can see what I saw.

"He flinched from doing his duty; he secured a victim and, by disfiguring this victim, sought to impress all concerned that it was he himself who had met that fate. He provided against the future by drawing twenty thousand pounds in gold. He sacrificed the rest of his property, for he dared not do otherwise. And even then, his fear of the vengeance of the club kept him from taking that twenty thousand from the portion due it.

"He is still in London, gentlemen. I have him located, for I followed him. He has broken the rules of the club, and the oaths he took. He is a traitor, and you know what must be done.

"Now then, gentlemen, prepare for the drawing, please. In a case of this kind, he who gets the black skull knows what is his duty, and let me say before the drawing, that duty must be performed without delay."

As he finished speaking, Palmer lifted the silver box and passed it to the man on his right, who pressed a tiny slide in the bottom and allowed something to drop into his hand. He then passed it on to the next, who did likewise, and in this fashion it passed down one side of the table and up the other until it had come back to Hammerton Palmer.

He then lifted it and did as the others had done, but, as he did so, there was one pair of eyes at that table which saw his fingers press a certain part of the box, and cause the thing which fell into his hand to drop from a different compartment than the one which had supplied the others.

Replacing the box on the table, Palmer again spoke.

"Gentlemen, table your draw, please!"

Instantaneously the right hand of each one at the table went down on the green baize, and remained in that position until Palmer said "Up!"

Then they were lifted, and on the green baize in front of each one was seen reposing a tiny skull. All but one were of pure white ivory. That one exception was of black ebony, and reposed in front of the man who had seen Hammerton Palmer take his skull from another compartment in the box.

To those at the table he was Number Seven; to Palmer himself he was supposed to be Graves; in reality, who had drawn the black skull which made him the instrument of vengeance against Number Six was Sexton Blake.

An involuntary sigh of relief went up from the others, and more than one sympathetic glance was thrown in the direction of Number Seven, who sat so impassive. Again Palmer spoke.

"Now, gentlemen, Number Seven has been drawn, and knows what he must do. We have still another draw, and then I shall release Number Seven. Before he goes, I shall tell him where to find Number Six. I trust it will not be his portion to again draw the black skull. Your skulls, please."

Each man passed along the skull which lay before him and, gathering them together, Palmer placed them back in the box.

"The next draw, gentlemen," he said, "is in regard to the man Sexton Blake. You will remember I said I had left a black skull with him. The first attempt to fulfil its sentence failed. The second must not. Prepare to draw, please."

Once more Palmer passed the silver box to the man on his right, and once more that member made his draw, passing the box on to the next. In the usual fashion it reached Number Seven, who had already drawn a black one.

So absorbed was each member in the draw that none had noticed the fingers of Number Seven as they sought the pocket of his waistcoat. Nor when the box came to him did they see the purpose of his clumsy draw.

If any did, he no doubt put it down to the nervousness on the part of Number Seven, from dread lest he should again draw a black one. Yet in the few moments during which the box had been in his hands, Number Seven had made the ordinary draw, and not only that, but his fingers had found the secret part pressed by Hammerton Palmer when he made his draw.

When his fingers had sought his waist-coat pocket, they had come away with the very black skull which had been left by Palmer in Sexton Blake's consulting-room, and before he passed the box on to his neighbour he had made his own draw, had pressed the secret part allowing the white skull which Palmer evidently took good care to assure to himself to drop into his hand, and had slipped into the secret compartment the black one he had taken from his pocket.

Then he passed the box on to his neighbour, and so, the draw continued until the box had once more reached the head of the table.

Following his former procedure, Palmer made his own draw, and placed the box on the table.

Then he repeated the words he had used before:

"Gentlemen, table your draw, please!"

Once again the right hand of each one at the table went up, and came down upon the green baize cover. Again Palmer's voice rang out:

"Up!"

Instantly every hand was lifted, and there reposing on the green cloth were the skulls. But this time there was a difference. Two, and not one, of the skulls were black. One black one lay in front of the apparently unlucky Number Seven, the other was in front of Hammerton Palmer.

But not for Number Seven were the eyes of the other members, even though for the second time he had drawn a black. Every man's attention was riveted on the masked countenance of their leader, and what a study in human expression it would have been could one have seen beneath those pieces of black silk!

Palmer was sitting rigid in his chair, his eyes glued upon the black skull in front of him. But though his features were masked, his hands were not, and all the control of the man could not keep them from trembling.

Involuntarily one of them went out towards the box as though to convince himself that he was not dreaming. How it had happened he did not know. Could he have taken his skull from the general compartment by mistake? No, that was impossible.

He was always too careful to arrange that his should come from the secret compartment, where only a white one reposed. Then, suddenly, his eyes fell on the other black skull in front of Number Seven, and he knew he had been duped.

For a moment he made as though to rise, then he sank back.

"Gentlemen," he said hoarsely, "I presume you have seen that there are two black skulls on the table. That means there is a traitor here amongst us. I demand that each one at the table shall unmask at once! Then we shall discover who that traitor is."

Immediately Palmer's hands and those of six others went up to their masks; but there were two who sat motionless. With a gesture Palmer checked the six.

"There appear to be two here who refuse to obey the order to unmask. Is it, then, that we have two traitors amongst us? I call upon you gentlemen to see that they obey the order!"

Just then he was interrupted by a low, ringing laugh. Every one at the table, even Number Seven, turned in the direction from which it sounded.

It had come from beneath the mask of a small, slim man at the far end of the table. According to the club record he was Number Two, and Number Two it was who, with Number Seven, had not obeyed the order to unmask.

Palmer uttered an angry exclamation, and started to rise. But whatever it was he intended doing was cut short for ever by a terrific explosion beneath their feet.

There was an infinitesimal instant of time while the roar sounded in their ears, then the walls of the room seemed to collapse like cardboard, the table heaved upwards, the ceiling dropped, and the nine human beings who a moment before had been sitting there so calmly became buried in a heap of debris. One or two cried out in terror, some moaned in agony, but for the most parts they lay still in the midst of the wreckage, deep in a sleep from which some of them would never awaken.

   •    •    •    •    •

Blake opened his eyes to find himself gazing up at the starlit sky. About him he could see several dark figures, while away over to the left was a great red glow.

Someone had an arm under his head, and had evidently been watching for his return to consciousness, for he saw the silhouette of a head as it bent over him, and felt the touch of a flask to his lips. Then he became conscious that a voice he knew well was talking to him softly.

"Are you feeling better now?" it said.

Making an effort, he twisted his head and found himself gazing up into Yvonne's eyes.

"What on earth has happened!" he muttered, straggling to a sitting position.

"Don't you remember the explosion and the collapse of the house?" asked Yvonne. "Someone blew it up."

Blake nodded.

"I remember now. It was right after you laughed out. I had no idea you were there until you did that. How on earth did you manage it?"

"I kidnapped a gentleman about my size who intended being there," said Yvonne. "He is now locked up in a room at Queen Anne's Gate, and I imagine when he hears what has happened, he will thank me. But how do you feel?"

"First rate. I am a little sore, but sound enough, I guess. What became of the others, and who got me out?"

"Two of the others have perished. Two are lying fatally injured, and two may recover. The bodies of the two who were killed were recovered, but only just in time. The house is in a mass of flames now. You can see it from here."

Blake gazed for a moment at the lurid spectacle. Then he turned back to Yvonne.

"You have not told me who got me out," he said slowly.

"Well —er —you see," she answered, "I was practically unhurt, and in the explosion you were thrown close to me. I managed to get you out a little way, and when the firemen arrived they got you clear."

Blake took her hand in his, and his voice was husky as he said:

"You try hard to gloss over your part in it, Yvonne. You need say no more. I know now to whom I owe my life.

"But for you I should have been lying now in the midst of those flames. But you have mentioned only six besides ourselves, Yvonne. That makes eight. There were nine in all. Is there one body which has not yet been recovered?"

She nodded.

"Yes."

"Do you know whose it was?"

"Yes," she whispered. "It was Hammerton Palmer's. But who could have committed the mad act of blowing up the place?"

"The act was mad, and the one who did it was mad," answered Blake. "I have a pretty good idea who it was, but if only I could find Tinker I should know for certain."

Scarcely had Blake finished speaking when there was a slight commotion on the outskirts of the crowd, and a dishevelled lad broke through.

"Is it the guv'nor?" he gasped, seeing Yvonne. "Oh, it is you after all, guv'nor!" he went on, when he saw Blake was conscious. "I have been searching for you everywhere. Are you badly injured?"

"No, my lad, thanks to Mademoiselle Cartier. But, tell me, have you any report?"

"Yes, sir —urgent!"

"Bend close and tell me what it is. Come here, Yvonne. I wish you to hear, too!"

Blake sat up and, though it was hardly necessary now, Yvonne still cradled his head against her arm. Tinker dropped on one knee and began speaking in low, rapid tones.

"I went to the London Docks right after dinner, guv'nor, and took up my watch. Nothing happened until about nine o'clock, when my man came out. He passed under a light close to me, and he did look wild about the eyes.

"I trailed him through the City, until we reached Park Lane. He hung about in the dark parts of the street for a bit, and while I was watching him, I saw several men enter the house you told me you were going to. That was also the one my quarry was interested in, the one which is burning now. I thought I recognised you as you went in.

"Well, sir, about ten-twenty my man got busy. He had been carrying a bulky parcel with him ever since he had started out, and seemed mighty careful of it. If I had only known what I do now, I —"

"Never mind, my lad," interrupted Blake impatiently. "What is done is done. The point is to strike while there is yet time. Go on!"

"Well, guv'nor, about ten-twenty he went up the steps and rang the bell. It was answered shortly, and after a long confab with the man who answered it, he was admitted.

"I stayed on the watch, and it was about ten minutes later that he came out again. I suppose he had persuaded the servant he had important business with his master, and that the servant allowed him to wait."

"Giving him time to fix his bomb," finished Blake.

"That's it, sir. Anyway, when he came out I started off after him. At Hyde Park Corner he took a taxi. I did so, too, and from there he was driven straight through to the London Docks.

"He got out near the docks, and walked on until he reached the old warehouse. I watched him until I saw a light go up, and then I made tracks back for Park Lane, never dreaming of what had happened since I had left.

"That is about all, guv'nor. When I reached here I discovered what had occurred. I knew you must have been in it, but could find out nothing. I have been searching everywhere for you. I forgot to say, sir, that when my quarry left the house here to return to the docks, he was without the package he had been carrying."

"There is no doubt but that it was the bomb which wrecked the place," said Blake. "It was mad —it was diabolical but he is still in London, and we must catch him."

"But who is he, Mr. Blake?" broke in Yvonne.

"Who is he?" repeated Blake. "He is the man who is supposed to have been murdered —Gilbert Jefferson. Come! We have no time to lose."

Disregarding all protests, Blake got to his feet and turned.

He found he had been carried on to a small grass plot in front of another house not far from the one where the explosion had occurred.

Tinker went ahead, and, as Blake and Yvonne followed, none guessed that the tall man who pushed his way through was one of those who had been in the house at the time of the explosion, or that the slim figure behind him had also been there, and that the long coat worn by the latter hid the figure of a girl.

Some distance down the street, Tinker succeeded in getting a taxi, and they climbed in. A few moments later, and they were out of the crowd, speeding towards London Docks.

Tinker gazed ahead eagerly, while Blake leaned back with a strange mixture of weariness and firm determination stamped on his features.

As for Yvonne, she gazed at Blake as a woman gazes at the man she loves when she thinks he may be suffering.

If he still felt any ill-effects from the explosion, Blake gave no sign as he stepped out of the cab at London Docks and gave his hand to Yvonne. Telling the driver to wait, he signed to Tinker to lead the way, and the three of them set off at a brisk pace in the direction of the old warehouse.

As they rounded the corner, Blake breathed more easily. A light still burned in the loft-room. They moved on until they reached the floor, and then, stepping forward, Blake raised his hand to knock, for he had no intention now of concealing his arrival.

But his hand never fell on the door, instead, he stepped forward with a low exclamation, and gazed into the dark recess before him with a puzzled frown. The door was wide open.

"Something has happened!" he said curtly, without turning. "Follow me!"

Drawing his revolver, he made his way through the doorway until his searching foot found the first step. Then he started up with Yvonne and Tinker close on his heels.

At the top he paused a moment. A thin crack of light ahead showed where the door of the room was. Blake started forward and, on reaching it, placed his hand on the latch. For a second he waited, then, raising his hand from the latch, he rapped.

At first he thought there was no answer, but a moment later he was sure he heard a low groan from inside. He waited no longer. Raising the latch he opened the door and entered.

Scarcely had he done so when he turned sharply and held out his arm to bar Yvonne's way.

"You mustn't come in," he said. "Something has happened."

But Blake's words were too late. She, as well as Tinker, had seen the huddled-up body on the floor by the table; had seen, as well, the small crimson pool on the floor, and had heard the groans which came from between the lips of the man who lay there.

After the first glance Blake hurried forward and, bending, lifted the man's head. Though he had expected to find the man he saw, he could not repress a slight thrill as he found himself gazing into the eyes of the man he knew to be Gilbert Jefferson.

All the madness had gone from them now. They were perfectly sane, and so was he, but the most inexperienced could have seen that he was doomed.

For a moment he gazed at Blake, and fear came into his eyes, as though he expected someone else; then, recognising a stranger, he whispered:

"Who are you?"

"I am, Sexton Blake, and you are Gilbert Jefferson, are you not?"

The stricken man nodded weakly.

"Yes. Will you take a confession before I die? I am done for."

"What do you wish to say —that you blew up Hammerton Palmer's house in Park Lane to-night?"

"My heavens! How did you know?"

"Never mind, Jefferson, how I know. You did, didn't you?"

"Yes."

"And it was you who killed the man at No. 12A, Fulton Terrace and, after disfiguring his features dressed him in your own clothes in order that he should be taken for you, wasn't it?"

"Yes —yes. But how do you know all this?"

"Don't waste time asking questions, man. You are done for, so answer mine and straighten things out as well as you can before you go. Was it through fear of the Death Club you did this?"

"Yes."

"Who was the man you killed?"

"A wharf labourer. He lived here. I met him and got him to call on me. After he came —I —killed —him!"

Blake had to bend very close, to catch the last few words, so weak had Jefferson's tones become. He signed to Tinker, who handed him a flask, and after he had forced a little brandy between Jefferson's lips, the latter again opened his eyes.

"You have been shot," said Blake slowly and distinctly, as soon as he saw the other could grasp what he was saying, "Who did it?"

Jefferson made a feeble gesture in the direction of the table.

"Hammerton —Palmer," he gasped. "Escaped —without — injury. —Must—known—where—I—was. —Came—on—at—once. —Said—all—others—been—killed. —He—and—I—last. Then— shot—me—left—paper—and—went—away. Don't—know—where. Curse—him—he—"

Then the voice trailed off and, with scarcely a shudder, Gilbert Jefferson was gone on his long journey into the unknown.

Blake laid him back gently and rose. He moved softly towards the table and searched for the paper Jefferson had said was there. He could hardly credit the fact that Palmer had escaped from the wrecked house; but he knew Jefferson had been perfectly clear in his mind at the last, and he had stated most definitely that Palmer had followed him on after escaping from the house.

Palmer's words to Jefferson, saying all the others had perished, fitted in with this, for if he had escaped and had hurried quietly away at once, he would know nothing about the work of rescue.

Underneath the bottle holding the candle, he finally spied a bit of paper. Drawing it out, he held it up, and as he saw what it contained, Blake knew Jefferson had told the truth —that Hammerton Palmer still lived.

On it was drawn a small black skull, nothing more. He had at last succeeded in carrying out the sentence of the Death Club which had been passed on Gilbert Jefferson.

And as he gazed at that small black skull, Blake remembered sentence which had been passed upon him. He wondered when and how he would again meet Hammerton Palmer.

## The Thirteenth Chapter.    Sexton Blake Relates His Case— The End.

Two hours after midnight that same night, there was a curious sextet of persons in the smoking-room of Yvonne's house at Queen Anne's Gate.

Firstly, there was Sexton Blake, seated at the desk facing the others, and smoking as nonchalantly as though he had never heard of a death club; secondly, there was Yvonne sitting very close to him, and still surreptitiously regarding him from time to time with a look from which all the tender anxiety was not yet gone.

Thirdly, there was Tinker, still appearing a little battered from his brush with the madman; fourthly, Graves was there, with a nervous look in his eyes; fifthly, Formby Mott, the lawyer; and sixthly, but by no means the least in evidence, was Inspector Thomas, wearing a very puzzled expression. That completed the party.

Immediately after the confession and death of Gilbert Jefferson in the old loft at the London Docks, Blake, Tinker, and Yvonne had hurried on to Queen Anne's Gate. From there Blake had summoned the lawyer and inspector, and they had arrived less than five minutes before.

Now they were waiting for Blake to speak —and speak he did.

"I presume you are wondering why I sent for you, inspector," he said, addressing the police official. "I shall not keep you in the dark. I sent for you to listen to the history of the Jefferson murder.

"I asked you to come, Mr. Mott, in order to hear what was paid for the sake of your client, Miss Alice Jefferson. Now, then, gentlemen, to begin.

"When I went with Inspector Thomas to No. 12A, Fulton Terrace, on the night of the murder, I outlined, as the inspector will recollect, several tentative theories as to how and by whom the murder was committed. All of us here are perfectly aware of the main clues in the case, so it will be unnecessary to make a detailed recapitulation of them.

"My theories, as dealt with that night, were more in the abstract, and not until Miss Jefferson called me in on the case did I begin to apply them where possible.

"It is needless to say that my first consideration was the mutilation by acid of the features and hands of the murdered man. To me, this seemed to be a very important point. I dealt with it in all its phases, and, after considering every point, I arrived at the conclusion that the chief motive for doing such a thing was exactly what the result showed—a mutilation of the features.

"For what reason? I asked myself. Two seemed more probable than any others. These two were, firstly, a brutal desire by the murderer to disfigure his victim; and, secondly, a wish to prevent the identification of the features of the murdered man.

"I took the latter as a working hypothesis, but by no means shelved the former. That was point one.

"My next effort was to discover the motive for the murder itself. I must confess that the first theory of robbery being the motive, appeared weak to me; but when I discovered from Mott about the twenty thousand pounds in gold which had been drawn from the bank and had disappeared, that theory was strengthened considerably.

"But even then I could not accept it, I will tell you why. My reason was that, from the fact that the features of the murdered man had been mutilated, I did not believe him to be Gilbert Jefferson. Already I felt that the latter was still alive.

"That was point two.

"My next move was to consider the two mysterious visitors who had been at the house on the night of the murder. Firstly, I went to the rear of the house, and there examined the footprints of the one who had been surprised by Sergeant Mullin and his men. I took impressions of these, measured their size, and the length of the stride, both running and walking.

"After the regular mathematical method of computation— a method with which the inspector is well acquainted —I concluded that the owner was either a misshapen man or a woman.

"Now, the sergeant would have noticed at once had the individual he surprised been misshapen. He made no mention of such a thing, so I felt fairly safe in assuming it to be a woman.

"That was point three.

"The next thing to be dealt with was the incident of the other caller. You will all remember the evidence of the butler. You will recall how a man, poorly dressed, called on Gilbert Jefferson that evening.

"You will remember that Jefferson sent the butler to bed, saying he himself would let his visitor out. You will also remember how the cook saw a man leave about ten-thirty.

"Everyone concluded that must have been the man who called on Jefferson. But already I was working on the theory that the murdered man was not Jefferson at all, and that he was still alive.

"Therefore, it was not a very far step to the elaboration of that theory in this way. Was it possible that the man who left about ten-thirty was Jefferson himself?

"Remember, the murdered man was wearing Jefferson's clothes, and the man who left was wearing the clothes of the man who had called. Therefore, if it was true that the murdered man was not Jefferson, and he was wearing Jefferson's clothes, I thought it very strong proof that the man who had left the house was Jefferson.

"That was point four.

"Now we come to the half-finished letter. That was accepted by all as being what it seemed —a letter being written when the writer was struck down.

"The writing was proved to be Jefferson's, yet, if he were still alive, he couldn't have been struck down while he was writing it. Therefore, I concluded it had been placed there in order to achieve the very purpose which it did achieve.

"By this time the whole case was dominated by Gilbert Jefferson. Consequently, when I considered the note which had been handed to the boy in Knightsbridge, it was not difficult to connect that as part and parcel of the letter scheme.

"If that man was Jefferson, he wished the police to come to the house in order that the morning papers might have a report of the murder.

"Why was that? What more likely than a very strong desire that someone should read of his death? And there I struck the first thing which seemed to point to the real motive for the whole affair.

"It was fear —deadly fear. Of whom was he afraid? I had no idea —then.

"After that I went over the terms of the will with great care. It was not until then that Hammerton Palmer appeared in the case, nor did he loom big in my calculations until after a conversation with Miss Jefferson over the telephone.

"Hard on that, Palmer came to see me, and when he had gone, any slight suspicion I may have had of him was deepened into certainty that he knew a great deal about the Jefferson affair.

"One reason was because I laid a trap for him, and without knowing it, he acknowledged that he knew death had been anticipated by Jefferson.

"Secondly, because after he left, I found this on my desk."

As he spoke, Blake drew from his pocket one of the black skulls, and laid it on the pad in front of him.

"Why, isn't, that the one you got from me?" asked the inspector quickly.

Blake smiled.

"Exactly similar, inspector, but not the same. Now to come to these skulls," he went on. "Mr. Mott may have wondered what became of one which he found amongst the belongings of Gilbert Jefferson. I plead guilty to the theft.

"When I saw it, my mind flew back to something the inspector had told me about the murder of Mr. Herbert Welkin, M.P. It was that a similar sort of skull had been found upon him.

"I slipped it in my pocket, and went to see the inspector. I found the one he had spoken of was exactly similar. This I procured from him, and when, after Palmer's visit I found one on my own desk, I immediately linked up Hammerton Palmer with the Welkin affair as well as the Jefferson case. Then it was that he dominated the case in my calculations.

"To proceed. That evening I went to see Miss Jefferson. Her first words were to tell me that she would be compelled to ask me to abandon my investigations. Naturally, I asked the reason.

"Her reply was to hand me a letter. It was a document from Gilbert Jefferson, charging her not to be a party to any investigations as to the cause of his death. It had been enclosed in an envelope bearing a typewritten address, and was accompanied by a note, also typewritten, which was unsigned, and purported to be from some individual to whom the document was given for safe keeping.

"She next handed me a letter which she had received from Hammerton Palmer. It was an urgent appeal to her to trust to him in her business dealings.

"Quite by chance I was led to scrutinise the address of this envelope, and was at once struck by its similarity to that on the other. I re-examined the other, and in two minutes I was certain both had been done on the same machine. Do you see how the arrow again pointed to Hammerton Palmer?

"Immediately after, she said she had noticed several people watching the house that evening. She spoke of a man in an ulster, who had been followed by a lad. I concluded, and rightly, that, whoever it was Tinker was on the trail.

"Then she spoke of a woman who was standing on a dark corner, watching the house. My mind leaped to the mysterious woman I had figured as being the owner of the footprints I had examined at the rear.

"I took my departure as soon as possible, but found she had gone. The lad who had been assisting Tinker, however, followed her, and brought me the information I needed.

"I interviewed her, and from her got a mass of valuable information. Then Tinker turned up, and from him I learned much more.

"After that, gentlemen, I made a good many researches into the life of Hammerton Palmer. I visited his offices, and by the use of strategy, got a sample of the work done by each of the typewriters there. From the one in his private office I got a sample exactly similar to the writing on the two envelopes addressed to Alice Jefferson.

"Now, to deal briefly with the information received from the woman the lad Tim had followed. For the present her name will not be mentioned. I discovered her interest in Gilbert Jefferson to be a business interest.

"I was certain all along that she had no connection with the murder, and that her presence there that night was a pure coincidence. I proved this to be so.

"But she had come upon a curious notice to a certain individual whose name also must remain with me for the present, to attend a meeting.

"After a full consideration of all the points, the chief of which was the fact that the notice had been written on the typewriter in Hammerton's office, I decided to attend this meeting.

"I attended the meeting, and, unknown to me, the woman who had been the means of discovering the meeting-place, attended it, too. Then the place was blown up.

"I have made out a full report of this meeting, and will hand it to Inspector Thomas.

"After that we hurried to the East End, where Tinker had followed the man in the ulster, and from where he had brought many articles which proved points which before had been doubtful.

"Not the least of these articles was a batch of half-finished letters similar to the one found on the desk at Fulton Terrace proving that Jefferson had practised on several before writing the one which was found.

"In the East End we found a man at the point of death. Before he expired, he acknowledged himself to be Gilbert Jefferson. He also confessed to the murder of the man at 12A, Fulton Terrace.

"Tinker took shorthand notes of this confession, and you will get it with the other document prepared for you. When asked who had shot him, Jefferson managed to tell me before he died.

"His murderer was Hammerton Palmer, the man I thought had perished in the explosion.

"That, inspector, is a general outline of the work I have done. Here, in a nutshell, is the final result of the case.

"Some five years ago Hammerton Palmer was a struggling stockbroker. He, in common with several others, made it a regular practice to gamble heavily at cards.

"It was then that a fiendishly brilliant idea struck Palmer. It was, that instead of gambling in the ordinary way, they should gamble in human lives.

"Palmer organised a club, known as the Death Club. Nearly every one of the men with whom he gambled became fascinated with the idea, and joined it.

"On joining, every member made a will leaving at least half his estate to some member of the club, and also left protective documents similar to those left by Jefferson.

"Once a month a meeting of the club was held. A silver box filled with tiny skulls was laid on the table. The skulls it contained were all white but one. That one was black.

"Then a draw took place, and the man who drew the black skull was doomed. He was given ten days in which to arrange his affairs, and then he was to commit suicide.

"When a man flinched from it, as did Herbert Welkin, M.P., another draw was made, and the man who drew the black skull this time was deputed to murder the man who had failed to do his part.

"Then, when the estate was settled, the club member who received the half-share, turned it over for an equal division amongst the members.

"Naturally, this sort of thing would soon depopulate the club, but Palmer provided against that. It was his custom to keep a careful look-out for City men who were on the brink of ruin through gambling in shares.

"He painted the thing in such colours to them that nine times out of ten they grasped eagerly at the chance to get back on their feet.

"That was how he caught Jefferson, and that was how Jefferson's financial condition improved so marvellously during the past seven months.

"It was bolstered up from the estates of other who had committed suicide, or had been murdered.

"Then came his turn. He realised what he had really entered into. He discovered that his own turn had come as sure as the wheel of Fate must turn.

"Like others, he flinched from paying the price. He racked his brains, and finally hit on a scheme which he calculated would let him off free, and still make the Death Club believe him to be dead. He elaborated his plan, and the murder at Fulton Terrace was the result.

"But you have all seen how his tracks were by no means completely obliterated, and that, consequently, not only was his guilt discovered, but the whole truth about the Death Club came out. One thing brought matters to a crisis to-night.

"Jefferson had drawn the twenty thousand pounds in gold in order to have a stake to begin anew in another country.

"It was his intention to leave England to-night, but something prevented. That something was the snapping of the man's sanity. The whole affair had unhinged his reason.

"Something whispered to him to destroy Palmer and the club before he went. He knew that the meeting was to be held, and forthwith proceeded to manufacture a bomb. He gained admittance to the house in Park Lane, placed his bomb, and escaped.

"But now we know that Palmer himself escaped. He guessed at once who was responsible for the explosion. In the report of the meeting of the club, inspector, you will see that he also knew by accident that Jefferson was alive, and where he was in hiding.

"He must have gone at top speed to the East End and shot Jefferson just before we reached there. At any rate, he is the man who has been the head and shoulders of the whole thing.

"And, moreover, he always provided for his own safety in the draw. He had a secret compartment made in the silver box, and from this he took his own draw. It was always white.

"The report also shows how I discovered this, and how I exposed his duplicity just before all my plans were shattered by the explosion. This, however, we know:

"Hammerton Palmer is the real author of many murders and suicides during the past five yeans. Hammerton Palmer is still at large.

"That is the story, inspector. That is your case. Here are the reports and proofs. He is your man. It is now up to you to find him."

For a long minute there was a heavy silence when Blake had finished his remarkable tale, Formby Mott was frankly dumbfounded at the insight he had just had into Blake's methods.

As for the inspector, he sat with wrinkled brows, pondering on what he had heard. Finally he looked up.

"You spoke of receiving some of your information about the Death Club from a woman, who, in turn, received it from member of the club," he said. "Are you determined to suppress her name and the name of the member?"

Blake smiled, and disregarded the inspector's glance in Yvonne's direction.

"Inspector," he said quietly, "the member who gave the information did so under my promise of protection. I can assure you that, although a member of the club, he has never had any criminal hand in its procedure. When you catch Palmer, he is prepared to come forward and tell what he knows.

"As for the woman's name, why, inspector, there isn't enough money in England to buy that information from me."

And from where he sat the puzzled inspector never saw the warm little hand which snuggled into Blake's as though content for always to rest secure in its protection.

THE END.
[58000 WORDS]

Sexton Blake realised that a voice he knew well was talking to him softly. "Are you feeling better now?" it said. Making an effort, he twisted his head and found himself gazing up into Yvonne's eyes. *(Chapter 12.)*

NEXT WEEK.

"The Lost King,"

The second tale of the series dealing with The Council of Eleven, in their efforts to win fortunes by means the Law does not acknowledge.

Your copy will cost you ONE PENNY, NEXT WEEK.